Creative Texts Publishers products are available at special discounts for bulk purchase for sale promotions, premiums, fund-raising, and educational needs. For details, write Creative Texts Publishers, PO Box 50, Barto, PA 19504, or visit www.creativetexts.com

CLAY BRENTWOOD: BOOK FIVE: THE STORM
by Jared McVay
Published by Creative Texts Publishers, LLC
PO Box 50
Barto, PA 19504
www.creativetexts.com

ISBN: 978-0-692-19753-0

THE STORM
By
JARED MCVAY

An imprint of Creative Texts Publishers, LLC
Barto, PA

This book is dedicated to all the wonderful western readers out there who take time from their busy schedules to relax with one of my books. Thank you for all your glowing reviews. You keep asking for more, I'll keep writing them. Through you, I gain new friends, daily. A word to my publisher, Dan Edwards at Creative Texts, thanks again for having faith in me as a storyteller. And to my right arm and faithful editor, Jerri Burr, without you I would be lost. Plus, you're a muy bueno mapmaker.

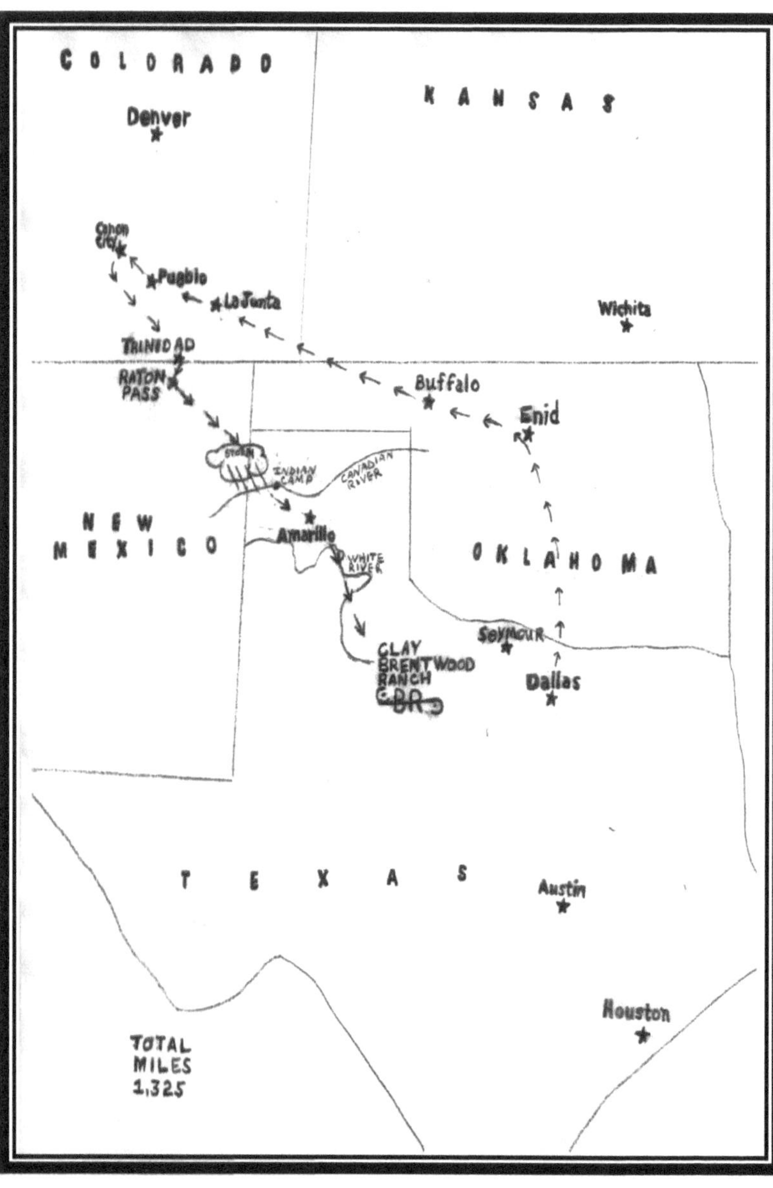
COLORADO
Denver
KANSAS
Cañon City
Pueblo
La Junta
Wichita
TRINIDAD
RATON PASS
Buffalo
Enid
STORM
INDIAN CAMP
CANADIAN RIVER
NEW MEXICO
Amarillo
WHITE RIVER
OKLAHOMA
Seymour
CLAY BRENTWOOD RANCH
CBR
Dallas
TEXAS
Austin
Houston
TOTAL MILES 1,325

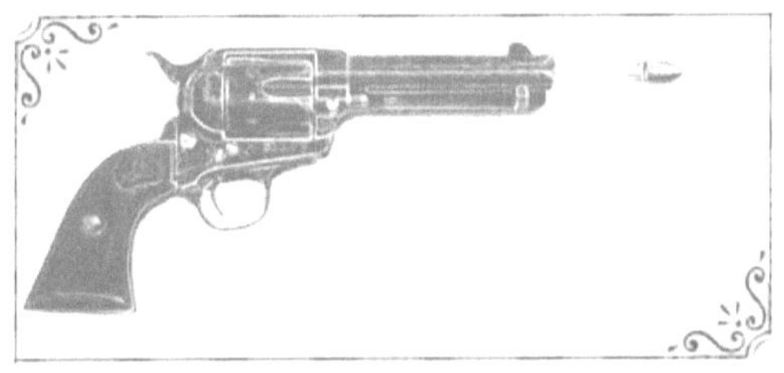

CHAPTER ONE

It was late afternoon when Little Joe Agular rode his stumbling horse into the yard and up to the front door of the small farmhouse where he slid off and dropped to the ground.

Alfred Carpenter and his wife, Pearl, ran out and looked down at a young man who was barely alive. He'd been shot in the backside of his left shoulder and had lost a lot of blood. His clothes were ragged, his face was streaked with sweat and dirt, and he had a gaunt look, like he hadn't eaten in some time.

Alfred and Pearl carried the young man into the house and laid him on the bed, then Alfred left his wife to see to the young man's wound while he went outside to tend to his horse, a brown and white paint – a mare about fourteen hands and not more than six years old by the look of her.

She was spent and barely able to stand. Her head was hanging down and her body was shaking like she was about to collapse. It was obvious she had been ridden long and hard without rest, and more than likely, no food or water.

Instead of trying to move her, Alfred went to the well and drew a bucket of water and set it in front of the horse's lowered head. "Try some of this, it'll make you feel better."

Smelling the water, she moved her mouth into the bucket and began to drink greedily, her body still trembling.

After a moment, Alfred gently lifted her head and said, "Just a little at a time, ole girl, just a little at a time, at least for now."

Very slowly, and with great patience, Alfred led the horse to the barn and put her in a stall, then added some hay and a bucket of oats to the eating trough, along with sitting the bucket of water nearby.

While she ate, Alfred stripped off her saddle and bridle, and then rubbed her down with a piece of burlap. Tomorrow he would see about her feet, but for now, she needed food and rest.

Alfred looked her over carefully and said to her, "At one time, not too long ago, you were in top shape or you wouldn't have been able to last as long as you did."

When he finished rubbing her down, she turned her head and looked at him with big, soft brown eyes as if to say, "thank you." Alfred smiled. "You'll be back on your feet in a day or two. All you need is some rest and food and water," he said, patting her gently on the neck before heading back to the house.

When he entered the bedroom, the young man was lying on their bed, face down and still unconscious. Pearl had just extracted the bullet from his shoulder with a pair of tweezers and held it up for her husband to see.

"Looks like he was running away from someone and was shot from behind," Pearl said. "And such a nice-looking young man, too."

Alfred nodded his head. "From the looks of his horse, he's been riding hard for some time. He must have been a very scared young man. He was fortunate his horse was in good shape. She's got sand, that one, but the poor thing wouldn't have made it another quarter of a mile."

"I wonder what happened? He looks so young and innocent," she said as she dabbed the wound with the same blue medicine they used on the horses to heal their cuts.

Using a dishtowel as a bandage, she bound up the wound and tied it in place as best she could. "That's the best I can do for now," she said. "I'll get some broth ready in case he wakes up."

Alfred studied the young man who was hanging onto life by a thread. He, too, wondered what had happened, but he wasn't so easily taken in by an innocent looking face, like his wife was. This was the west and just because he had an innocent look about him, didn't mean he was a church choirboy. He came in riding a horse he'd run to the ground, and he was dressed in town clothes with high top shoes, which told him the young man wasn't a farmer or a cowboy, but that was all.

He'd been shot from the back, which probably meant he was trying to get away from somebody. They had found no money on him, nor was he carrying even one piece of identification on him. There was nothing that could tell them who he was or where he was from – which out here was not unusual. Many of the men out here couldn't read or write, so they gave little attention to carrying identification. Who a man had worked for carried most of the weight when looking for a job.

If they knew their name and where they were from, that was enough. As long as you kept your nose clean, people didn't pry.

The fact that he had no weapon or money on him, added to the mystery. So, what had he been running from, and why?

Alfred walked into the kitchen and poured himself a cup of coffee. Maybe the young man would give them some answers when he woke up, if he ever did. He'd lost a lot of blood and in Alfred's opinion, it could tell, it could go either way.

Pearl finished doing her best to make the young man comfortable, then placed a blanket over him and began wiping the dirt from his face with a wet cloth when Alfred walked out onto the front porch and looked in the direction of the cornfield. The late afternoon sun was descending toward the west, disappearing behind the tall stocks of corn.

It was early fall and Oklahoma was nice this time of year. He was glad he and Pearl had left Iowa and come to Oklahoma two years ago. They would have a chance here, where they wouldn't have had back in Iowa. Those bible thumpers back there would never have allowed them to be happy. Not that he didn't believe in God, they both did, but neither her family nor his, wanted them to get married and had been vocal about it. In fact, his father had vowed to disinherit him if he married Pearl, just because she was Catholic and they were hardcore Baptist.

He and Pearl loved each other and that was all that mattered, but the narrow-minded Iowans couldn't seem to understand that.

"Ya just don't mix religions," his pa had said. "And you'll listen to what I'm sayin', if you ever want to inherit this place someday."

Alfred looked at his father and instead of anger - he felt pity for him. "You don't have anything I want, Pa. Give it to your precious church. I'm leavin'. I'll be gone by noon."

His mother cried when he left, but his father yelled at him, "You'll rot in hell. Mark my words, you and that Catholic bitch will both rot in hell!"

As he thought back, the only good memory he had was that he'd learned to grow corn and raise cattle from the man. When his father wasn't farming, he was a part time hell fire and brimstone Baptist preacher. Anyone who wasn't a part of how he believed was a sinner and headed straight for hell. Alfred felt no anger toward them, only pity.

Well, that was all behind them now. They had a nice piece of land here in Oklahoma, not far from Enid, where he could grow a crop and had plenty of pasture to raise a few cattle. He looked forward to a long and happy life here. The bull he'd recently purchased would help increase his small herd and Pearl had recently told him she was in the family way. Life was good.

If only Alfred had the ability to see into the future, he would have loaded the young man into his wagon and taken him straight to the sheriff in Enid, but Alfred was not blessed with that ability.

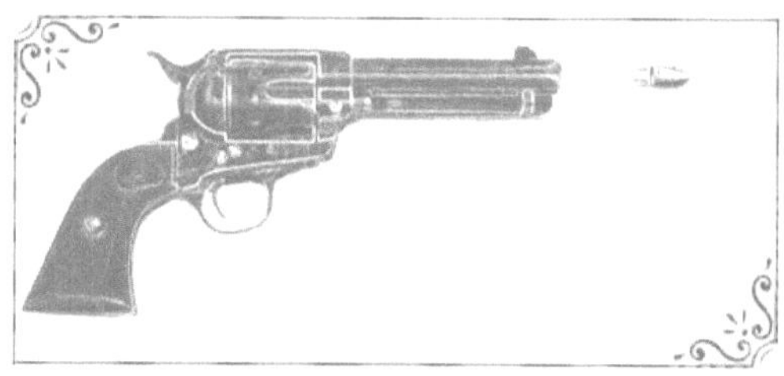

CHAPTER TWO

-

Clay Brentwood stepped out of the hotel and stood on the sidewalk, feeling clean and invigorated for the first time in six months. The Eaton Hotel had provided him with a long, leisurely hot bath, where he lounged for close to an hour with a cigar and two cold glasses of beer, along with getting a haircut and a shave. He was wearing a brand-new black hat, a new black suit, and a new pair of boots along with other new articles of clothing.

Technically, he was still a Texas Ranger for another year and Bill McDaniel, head of the Texas Rangers, was still his boss, but Bill had given Clay time off to recuperate from his wounds and rebuild his ranch. He was on what you might call, an as needed basis.

During the Cinch Mountain incident, Silas Mullin had tied him up and hung him from a tree limb and cut his back to ribbons with a blacksnake whip, and during the shootout that followed he wound up with several other cuts and contusions.

By the time Loralie Benson got her land back, Clay was ready for some time away from chasing bad men, and or, women. He was beginning to think he just might have more scars on his body than any five men should have.

After the Cinch Mountain incident, he'd taken the train to Wichita where he'd purchased the material he needed to rebuild his ranch house, barn and other buildings, down in Texas. He also hired eight carpenters - experienced builders who could build what he wanted built, the way he wanted it built. That had been six months ago. The work had gone well and he was very pleased with what they had created.

Now he was back in Wichita and had purchased a thousand head of short horned cattle. Yesterday he'd hired six wranglers to drive the cattle back down to Texas.

By now, it was October and his time to move them was getting short. The weather in this part of the country was still fairly decent, but he knew it could change at any time.

On the corner, Clay stopped and stood looking at the traffic going up and down the street. Wichita was no longer the wild cow town that had been written about in the dime novels.

Wyatt Earp, Doc Holiday and the others were now only a part of Wichita's past. For the most part there was law and order now, although Wichita was still far from tame.

Wichita was becoming an important city. There was a new flourmill going up that would produce a hundred barrels a day. There was a stove and ironworks plant, a meat packing plant, and a control center for the railroad. A new cold storage company had just opened its doors, and the Wichita Eagle newspaper was becoming a major news operation; along with the fact that the city could now boast of a school of higher learning, the newly built Fairmount College, and thirty miles to the east, oilrigs could be seen dotting the landscape.

Clay's attorney, Fredrick Blackstone, had made several wise business decisions which made sure Clay would never have to worry about money ever again, along with putting a hefty fee into his own bank account. The biggest coup being the sale of Clay's bank, The People's Bank, to the Kansas National Bank, where Clay received a sizeable sum of money to add to what he already had, plus becoming a major stockholder in the new bank. Clay still owned over a thousand acres of land and three local businesses; a saloon, a building that housed a doctor's office, a dental office and the office of his attorney, along with the building that he rented to the Wichita Eagle newspaper.

By anyone's standards, Clay Brentwood was a wealthy man, which in fact he was, but not by his own doing. If not for his father-in-law and his wife, who had both gone to meet their maker, he would still be just a man trying to build a dream.

His father-in-law had been the one with the business sense and had built up a fortune, which had passed on to Clay's wife when he died; then it passed on to him after the Beeler gang murdered her. And now, with his attorney looking after things, his wealth just kept growing. He would give up all the money if he could get them back, even for one day, but that was only a dream that could never come true.

Clay dropped the butt of his cigar onto the wooden sidewalk and snubbed it out with the toe of his boot. He and Fredrick Blackstone were going to the funeral of the former Kansas National Bank president, J. Oaks Davidson, who had died of a heart attack a few days ago.

Clay was about to step off the sidewalk when a commotion across the street drew his attention.

A man came backing out of the bank holding a young woman by her arm. The man was brandishing a pistol and yelling, "I see anybody comin' after us, she dies!"

Two men carrying saddlebags and waving their pistols around, ready to shoot anyone who opposed them followed the man out to where three horses stood at the hitch rail.

The first man forced the girl to climb up onto the saddle, then mounted behind her, while the other two men mounted their horses, looking this way and that in case anyone tried to interfere with the bank robbery, but no one made an attempt to stop them.

With a yell, they started down the street, kicking their horses in the sides and firing their pistols in the air.

"So much for Wichita becomin' civilized," Clay said to no one in particular.

Clay's first instinct was to draw his pistol and shoot the bank robbers as they went by, but there was the girl and she might catch a stray bullet. Instead, Clay leaped onto the hitch rail and launched himself at the first outlaw as he came riding past.

Since they were watching the street behind them, no one saw Clay until he slammed into the lead outlaw with his shoulder and drove him from his saddle.

The outlaw let out a yell and dropped the reins of his horse as he went airborne, leaving the girl to deal with the now racing horse.

Apparently, she knew something about horsemanship because before the reins could hit the ground and possibly cause the horse to stumble, she reached down and grabbed

them, then turned the horse off to the side and hauled him up short – out of the line of fire.

Luckily, Clay landed on top of the outlaw, cushioning his fall. As he rolled off, a bullet slammed into the dirt near his head and another one tore a hole in his new suit coat up near the shoulder and he felt a searing pain as the bullet ripped a groove in the upper part of his arm.

Clay continued to roll, dropping his hand to his pistol and bringing it into action. As fast as he could squeeze the trigger, his pistol sent two death warrants into the chests of the other two bank robbers, knocking them from their saddles. The dust hadn't settled yet when Clay swung his pistol toward the first outlaw who lay blankly staring at the sky, his head at a funny angle. The man's neck had been broken in the fall.

Clay stood up and began dusting off his new suit that was now covered with dirt and horse manure from rolling in the street.

Plus, a trail of blood was seeping from his wound, staining his new jacket. "So much for a bath and clean clothes," he said as he looked around for his hat, which had come off during the fight. It was laying in the street where it had been trampled by the horses. After dropping his pistol into his holster, he picked up his hat and dusted it off, trying as best he could to reshape it before putting it back on his head, but wasn't very successful. It was still dirty and rumpled.

People were crowding around, talking in hurried tones and gaping at the three dead bank robbers lying in the street, and then up to the young lady who was still sitting on the horse. Her eyes were wide with excitement.

Mister C. H. Davidson, son of the recently departed, J. Oaks Davidson, came to a halt near where Clay was standing, "Are you alright, Mister Brentwood?"

After his father passed on, as vice president of the bank, C. H. moved into his father's position of president and was concerned over Clay's well-being.

Clay grinned and said, "Other than smellin' like the inside of a barn, ruinin' my new suit and havin' ah gunshot wound in my shoulder, I guess I'll live ta see another day."

Before the new bank president could say anything else, the recently appointed marshal of Wichita, L. A. Knight, and two of his deputies, came running up pointing shotguns at Clay.

"With two fingers, lift that widow maker out of the holster, real easy like, mister, and drop it to the ground, then grab some sky!" Knight yelled.

Knight was a big man, well over two hundred pounds and taller than Clay by a head. He had a bushy moustache, several days of beard and green eyes that showed no humor.

His two deputies were hard looking men, more than likely hired for their fighting abilities. Clay knew their kind and decided not to antagonize them. As keyed up as they were, it wouldn't take much for them to start blasting away. Being loaded down with buckshot, especially when he hadn't done anything wrong, was no way to die.

Clay couldn't blame the marshal for being cautious. After all, he more than likely hadn't seen what happened, and had only been alerted that something was up when he heard the gunshots, and he wasn't about to take any chances until he got things figured out.

C. H. Davidson stepped off the sidewalk and walked up to the marshal. "You've got this all wrong, Lonny," he said to the marshal. "This is Mister Clay Brentwood. Those men on the ground robbed the bank and Mister Brentwood shot it out with them," he said, waving his hand in the direction of the dead men. "Mister Brentwood is not an outlaw - no sir, not by a long shot. Not only is he a major stockholder in the bank, he's also a business man, a rancher, and a Texas Ranger!"

L. A. Knight looked at Clay and asked, "That true, you're a Texas Ranger?"

"Guilty," Clay said, casually. "And if you'll permit me, I'll reach inta my shirt pocket and get my badge."

"Go ahead," the marshal said, but kept his shotgun at the ready.

After hearing what had happened, the marshal ordered the three bodies to be taken down to the undertaker, then apologized and offered to buy Clay a drink, thanking him for what he'd done. Along with most of the town, he also had money in the bank and didn't like the thought of some bank robbers riding away with it, plus taking a woman with them. Women were scarce enough as it was, and this one was pretty.

Clay thanked the marshal, but declined, saying, "I think I need ta see about my arm, then get a bath and inta some clean clothes before I do much socializin'."

They both laughed, then shook hands.

Clay headed for the doctor's office to see about his wound. He would miss the funeral but that was to be expected.

Two hours later, Clay stood in front of the mirror in his hotel room, dressed in clean jeans and a clean shirt. He'd decided against another new suit, at least for now. His new boots had come through it all no worse for wear and the owner of the mercantile store sent over a new hat, his compliments for stopping the holdup. Clay strapped on his six-gun and decided he was once again fit to go out in public.

Wichita had a no wearing or carrying of guns inside the city limits law, but being a law officer, the law didn't apply to him.

Before leaving his room, he looked at his pocket watch and saw it was coming up on suppertime, which was the reason for his growling stomach. Plus, he had six wranglers to feed.

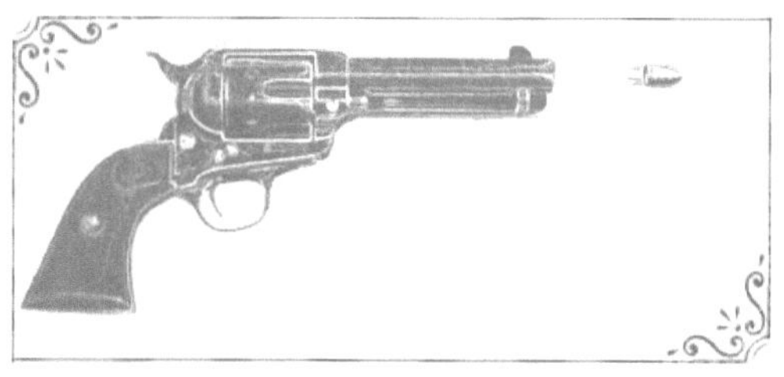

CHAPTER THREE

-

When Clay came down the front stairs of the hotel, he saw the young woman who had been taken hostage by the bank robbers. She was standing in the lobby of the hotel, looking in his direction. Next to her stood an older woman, maybe fortyish, who by all appearances was probably the young woman's mother. There was a strong family resemblance and both, were very attractive.

Taking off his hat, Clay walked over and asked, "Are you all right?"

The young woman blushed and said, "Yes sir, Mister Brentwood. I'm fine. I've been riding since I was very young, so I had no difficulty with the horse. It was the thought of what those men might do that worried me." After a moment, she looked up at him and said, "I want to thank you for saving me from those awful men. I don't know…"

Clay raised his hand and said, "No thanks necessary, I did what needed ta be done, considerin' the situation. I'm just glad you're all right."

She was of medium height, slender, with a nice figure. She had dark brown hair and soft brown eyes, and a smile that lit up the room. Clay was sure she turned a lot of heads when she walked down the street.

The girl was a younger version of her mother, who was making harrumphing noises.

The young lady's face turned a crimson color and she said, "Oh, please excuse my rude manners. I guess I was caught up in what you did for me. My name is Cindy McIntyre and this is my mother, Colleen McIntyre."

Clay shook hands with her mother, then asked if they'd had supper yet.

"Oh, it's not imposin' on ye we'll be doin'. But it's thankin' ya, we are," Colleen McIntyre said.

Clay felt embarrassed. "I'm sorry, I suppose your husband will be expectin' you home soon."

"My dear father was killed two years ago, back in Pennsylvania. He worked the coal mines and there was a cave in," Cindy said. "My mother and I are just passing through. We're looking for work and we stopped at the bank to see if they knew if anyone was hiring. I guess we should have waited a bit longer before going in or maybe gone to the newspaper."

Clay nodded and then asked, "What kind of work are you lookin' for?"

"If I may be so bold," Cindy said, "my mother is a superb cook; as good as any fancy chef with his big hat and all. You know, the kind that ya see in them big city restaurants, and we also do house cleaning and laundry, along with any mendin' that might need doin'."

Clay's eyes shifted toward the older woman and saw her face turning red. "Is that true? You're a superb cook?" he asked with a grin.

The woman raised her head and looked Clay in the eyes and said, "Well now, I wouldn't be knowin' about the superb part, but I've never seen the man yet who turned away from me table. And as far as the rest, well... I suppose that part is true, we do cleanin' and mendin' and such."

"Then I insist we have supper together and I'll not take no for an answer. We have much ta discuss," he said, taking both their arms.

After getting his crew down at tables and telling the waitress to bring their bills to him, he walked over and sat down with Colleen McIntyre and her daughter.

Over supper, Clay hired them both to do the cooking and cleaning and the running of his ranch house down in Texas. They would have their own quarters and be in full control of the house.

Clay could see the eagerness in their eyes and raised his hand.

Before allowing them to accept the jobs, he decided to explain to them what they'd be facing.

"The closest neighbor is Marion and Rebecca Sooner. They're real nice folks but they live several miles away. The closest town where you can shop is Seymour, fifteen miles to the east. You'll be livin' on ah ranch, ah long way from any neighbors or towns. It will be ah hard, lonely life, especially being the only females on the place with ah bunch of men not yet trained in the ways of being around the gentler sex."

Cindy's mother smiled, and said, "It's thankin' ya we are for the warnin', but ye'll no be worrin' ahboot us. They can't be no worse than a bunch of Pennsylvania coal miners. We'll be fine Mister Brentwood. Now, is there anything else we need ta know?"

Clay looked at the two women he'd just hired and smiled. With the ranch taking shape and men working it, they would need a cook, so why not a pretty one who could cook, instead of some ole wrinkle faced cowboy too old to do any wrangling, who couldn't cook anything but beef and beans, like the one they'd had during the rebuilding.

"We like our coffee hot and strong," Clay said as he took a bite of his steak.

The following morning, Mrs. McIntyre and her daughter went to the mercantile store and picked out things they would need, including certain women things, charging it all to Clay's account.

While they were doing that, Clay purchased a chuck wagon and six oxen to pull it, along with a smaller covered wagon and a team of four horses. The smaller wagon was for the women to sleep in, along with carrying their personals. Since both said they could drive the teams, he allowed that Mrs. McIntyre would drive the chuck wagon and Cindy would drive the other one.

It would be difficult driving a large herd with only six men and himself, but in two or three days, once the cattle got used to the drive and settled in, six wranglers with good horses would be enough. White face cattle were a lot easier to move than mossy ole long horns that were ill tempered and always on the prod.

Wranglers usually needed at least six horses to switch to during the drive and three of the wranglers had their own string, which Clay paid extra for, along with buying more to fill out the remuda. When they got back to the ranch, they could capture wild horses to add to the herd, but for now these would have to do.

At first, the men grumbled about it being bad luck to have a woman on a cattle drive, let alone, two; but after the first day, to the man, they all changed their minds. Food is important to a cowboy, especially on a cattle drive. So, when they stopped that first day and went to the chuck wagon for the noon meal, they were in for a surprise. There was beef stew, laced with vegetables that melted in their mouths, homemade soda bread with slabs of butter and apple pie with thick cream. Not only was the food better than any food they'd ever had on a trail drive, the women were pleasant to look at and old superstitions were forgotten faster than the blink of an eye.

With decent weather and good conditions, meaning no trouble with rustlers or Indians, Clay figured the trip should take about twenty to twenty-five days. If Clay wanted to push them, he could get twenty-five miles a day, but that would run off a lot of weight and they would be irritable and hard to handle. But, if they took their time and allowed them to rest and graze at noontime, they could do fifteen miles a day without worrying too much about weight loss.

CHAPTER FOUR

-

It was late afternoon of the first day and they were still several miles inside the Kansas border, when Clay found a place to camp for the night, near a small lake that would provide enough water for the herd. They would have to camp out in the open, but the weather was decent enough so that it shouldn't be a problem. By tomorrow noontime, they should reach the Panhandle of Oklahoma where water was scarce.

Clay didn't want to push the herd too hard. He wanted them in good shape because it would be at least two more days before they could reach the Cimarron River and cattle don't travel well without water.

He figured they would lose a little weight during the three-hundred-and-fifty-mile drive, but once they got to his land, it wouldn't take them long to put the weight back on. The White

River ran through his property with several small tributaries, and there was plenty of tall grass.

The cattle weren't used to walking all day and were more than ready to settle down for the night when the time came.

No one knew how Mrs. McIntyre did it, but that evening for supper, they feasted on corned beef and cabbage with soda bread and large slabs of butter, and blackberry pie. She'd seen some blackberries growing wild and since the herd was moving slow, she'd stopped and picked enough for six pies.

"Ya know, boss," Riley, a tall young man from Texas, said, "if this is the way we're gonna eat, I don't reckon you'll ever be wantin' fer hands. Women or not, this is the best trail drive I've ever been on, and if my work suits ya, I'll be stayin' on when we get to yer ranch."

Riley was young, just seventeen, but he'd been around cattle drives most of his young life and he knew his business. Clay was lucky to have him. Young he might be, but Clay was guessing the young man would ride for the brand, should trouble arise.

Clay looked out across the herd and watched as his men worked the cattle. There was a mixture of ages, which was good as far as he was concerned. The men new to this kind of work would learn from the more experienced riders.

Bert, a young man of twenty, from Arkansas, who was still learning about cattle drives, but worked hard, walked up to Colleen, doffed his hat and said, "Ma'am, if this is the way we'll be eatin' onect we get to the ranch, I reckon I can speak fer all of us and say, we ain't never leavin'."

Colleen blushed and waved the end of her apron at him. "Ah, go on with ya now. You and yer silver tongue. Ah man works hard, he needs ah good meal, that's all."

Bert took his slice of blackberry pie and backed away, saying, "Yes ma'am. Whatever you say, ma'am."

After the evening meal, Cindy brought out her guitar and sat on the tailgate of the wagon and to everyone's surprise, began to strum a slow, song of home. Then she began to sing and as if by magic, the cattle settled down.

Singing was what cowboys did while riding night herd to help keep the cattle calm, but none of them had a voice as soothing as Cindy McIntyre.

Clay had just poured himself a cup of coffee and was enjoying Cindy's singing, when a young man came riding up to the camp and got down. He took a double take when he saw the two women, then spied Clay and walked up to him. "Mister Brentwood?"

Clay smiled. He was just a boy, no more than fourteen and dressed in town clothes. "Sorry son, but I got all the wranglers I need."

The boy grinned. "I'm not a cowboy, sir. I'm Ben Masterson and I work for the railroad. I'm training to be a telegraph operator."

"I see," Clay said, getting a rumbling feeling in his stomach. "So, what brings you way out here?"

"A telegram, sir. I have a telegram for you. Sam, the telegraph operator, said he thought I could catch you if I rode hard," Ben told him, holding up a yellow piece of paper.

Clay wasn't sure he wanted to know what the telegram said, but took it anyway. Clay pulled out a dollar and handed it to the young man. "Here, take this, and thank ya for ridin' all this way. Go on over to the chuck wagon and tell Mrs. McIntyre to give you some supper."

When the boy left, Clay took his coffee and walked over and squatted down next to the fire. He stared at the telegram for a long while before turning it over and reading it. It was addressed to him alright.

GO TO DALLAS: SEE SHERIFF:

ESCORT MAN TO CANON CITY, COLORADO

PRISON: FOR EXECUTION:

The telegram was signed by Bill McDaniel, head of the Texas Rangers.

Clay wrote his reply on the back of the telegram with a pencil the young man furnished, briefly stating he would be in Dallas in about a week to ten days, then paid the young man for the telegram and told him he could spend the night and go back to Wichita come morning, which the young man agreed to, saying he didn't like riding in the dark.

Clay decided he would stay with the herd until they got down into Texas. When he figured they had a straight shot, he would draw a map for Riley, who knew more about Texas than the others, then he would head on down to Dallas. He looked at the sky and wondered why the rangers had gotten the job of taking a prisoner to Colorado and why he'd been chosen to do the escorting?

The following day, the tension of having women along eased up and that night when Cindy brought out her guitar and began to play and sing, the men relaxed right along with the cattle.

In the beginning, Clay wondered if it would be safe to have women along on the drive, suspicion being what it was, but he had chosen good men who rode for the brand and knew what would happen if any one of them got out of line. Women were scarce and nothing but a low life would mistreat one. And when he was caught, which he would be, he would rue the day, knowing he would suffer a slow, torturous death – being shot or hung would be too quick. Women molesters were thought to be lower than horse thieves and a horse thief was about as low you could get.

Clay was feeling the relaxation of the music and was about to lie down on his bedroll and try to get a little sleep when he heard the yell and all hell broke loose.

There was not only yelling, but several men were shooting pistols and he felt the earth tremble as the herd began to move.

"Damn," he yelled… They were on the outskirts of the badlands of Oklahoma and he'd not taken that into consideration. The badlands were where outlaw gangs hid out and a cattle drive was like waving a licorice stick in front of a young boy.

As he jumped to his feet and ran for his horse, he noticed both women had appeared, holding rifles in their hands.

"The camp will stay safe, Mister Brentwood," Colleen called out as Clay swung aboard the black stallion. The other wranglers were already chasing after the herd.

Clay nodded, knowing she was right, then let the black stallion have his head.

In the moonlight, he could see five men - all yelling and swatting at the cattle, urging them into a full stampede.

Clay's men were trying to outrun the stampeding cattle and turn them and hopefully slow them down, along with shooting at the outlaws, but getting the cattle slowed down would be the number one priority. The ones trying to turn the herd knew the others would be dealing with the cattle rustlers.

One of the rustlers was raising a rifle to his shoulder, pointing it in the direction of Riley. Clay pulled his own rifle from its boot and threw it to his shoulder and squeezed the trigger. There was a loud boom, and when the smoke cleared, Clay saw an empty saddle.

He was looking for his next victim when a bullet tore a hole through the crown of his new hat.

He swung his rifle and saw the outlaw raising his rifle for another shot when he fired and emptied the second saddle.

One of the rustlers tried to turn his horse in order to flee, but the horse stumbled and the man was thrown out into the stampeding herd. Clay heard him scream as several of the running cattle stepped on him and tripped, causing a pileup from behind, helping to slow the herd down.

Clay saw the last two rustlers racing away at breakneck speed into the safety of the night, and lowered his rifle. They were already too far away for a clean shot.

By then, his riders had turned the herd and they were slowing down, some two miles farther across the prairie.

When it was all said and done, they had lost three head, but gained three horses and rigs. They buried the rustlers all in the same hole and no words were said over them. They tried to steal what wasn't theirs and paid the price.

After the cattle were, for the most part, lying down and resting, they rode into camp to see if there might be some coffee.

To their surprise, not only was there fresh coffee, but also bacon and flapjacks, with a large bowl of butter and sorghum molasses.

"Well now, that was ah bit of excitement we didn't need, did we?" Colleen said as she poured Clay a cup of steaming coffee. "After all that hard ridin' I'm thinkin ye might have worked up ah bit of an appetite."

"You'll do ta ride the river with," Clay said as he loaded his plate.

Colleen and Cindy stood to the side, smiling with pride as each man doffed his hat and said, "Thank you," as they walked passed.

When everyone had a plate filled with flapjacks and bacon, Colleen walked over and stuck her finger in the hole of Clay's new hat. "Tsk, tsk, tsk, and ah new hat ta boot. Let me have it and I'll see what I can do." And with that, she disappeared inside the second wagon.

While they ate, Clay went over the rest of the trail in his head. Other than Indians, and he had an idea for that should they show up, the rest of the trip should go smoothly as long as the weather held. The land would be reasonably flat and there would be water and grass enough.

By the time Clay finished eating and was putting his plate into the tub of dishwater for Cindy to wash, Colleen came waltzing up with Clay's hat and handed it to him.

Clay's eyes got big and he grinned from ear to ear. The hole was gone and, in its place, a white star had been weaved into the material. And from what Clay could judge, the hole had been dead center of his hat, so the star looked as though it belonged there.

By the time the sun came up, the cattle had rested and Clay was getting restless and told them it was time to move out.

"We're not out of the woods just yet," he told them. "We're still in the badlands. I doubt we'll see any more rustlers, but we need ta keep an eye out. And we still have Indian country ta go through."

The days were long and dusty, but they'd had no more trouble except for cattle that were tired of traveling and either wanted to lay down and rest or run away.

Toward the end of day six, Slim, who was riding point, raised his arm in the air and pointed off to his left.

Slim was a long drink of water who had been over the mountain a couple of times and was a good man to have on the drive. He was close to forty who knew his business and didn't panic easily.

Clay rode up next to him. The sun was still up, but headed toward the horizon - its rays shining brightly on the small group of Indians sitting astride their horses off to the left, on top of a small rise.

"What'ya think, boss?" Slim asked.

"For now, keep the herd movin' just like we have been. I'll see if they'll palaver."

Clay cut from the herd and headed in their direction at a slow, easy walk. He was riding a sorrel mare who could run all day if he needed her to, and he had his pistol and rifle.

When the Indians saw a man riding toward them, a tall, rawboned warrior who was called Blue Coat because of the blue uniform jacket he'd taken during a battle eased his horse down the hill.

As they got closer, Clay could see the Indian was part of the Shawnee Nation and he knew he needed to be cautious. The Shawnee were noted to be fierce warriors and this one looked like he had plenty of experience along those lines.

When they met, somewhere in the middle, they sat staring at each other for some time before Clay raised his arm in the sign of peace.

Blue Coat studied this white man who dared to ride out alone, but said nothing, nor did he raise his arm in the sign of peace.

Clay knew he could show no weakness for if there was one thing an Indian hated, it was weakness. He had planned for this, but whether it would work or not was something yet to be seen.

Clay took his time and rolled a cigarette and lit it, blowing the smoke off into the evening sky, then said, "We are just travelin' through, but if your people are hungry, I can spare five head of cattle," hoping the man understood English.

"Twenty," Blue Coat said, speaking very good English.

Clay knew he was being put to the test and looked the man straight in the eye. "I said five. That's all I will give."

"What if we take? We are twenty and you are only seven. Plus, I may want the women for myself," he said with a leer. "I am Blue Coat of the Shawnee and I do not bow to any white man," he said, banging his chest with his fist.

Well, there it was, Clay thought. This Blue Coat had thrown out a challenge as plain as if he had drawn a picture.

Clay snubbed out his cigarette between his thumb and forefinger, then tossed the remains to the wind.

"I reckon we're at an impasse," Clay said. "You don't want ta give in ta me and I ain't gonna give in ta you, so what do you suggest?"

Blue Coat studied Clay's eyes and saw no fear. This one would not scare, he thought to himself, which suited him just fine. A thought that came into his mind and he smiled.

"We fight," Blue Coat said, matter of factly, watching for the white man's reaction.

"Your warriors against me and my men?" Clay asked.

Blue Coat grinned for the first time. "No, white man - just you and me - here and now, with knives. After you are dead, I may let the others live to tell of Blue Coat's fierceness, but I will take the women and all of the cattle."

Clay sighed. Would there ever come a time when men would settle their grievances by playing checkers, or some other non- violent means? He doubted it.

"If I win, you leave with no cows. If you win, you get twenty cows and leave us alone."

Blue Coat slid off his horse and stood looking at Clay, making no concessions, and after a moment, he drew his knife and motioned for Clay to get off his horse.

"I could shoot him and run for it, but we'd have to fight the rest of them and I can't take the chance with the odds in their favor. Besides, who knows how many head of cattle they'd run off," Clay whispered to himself.

Clay's men and the two women watched as Clay stepped down and took off his gun belt and hung it on the saddle horn, then removed his shirt and hat and laid them over the saddle.

"What the hell does he think he's doin'?" Bert asked.

Slim spat a long stream of tobacco juice into the dust and said, Indians only respect one thing and that's bravery. Looks like that Indian challenged the boss and he accepted."

"What will happen now?" Cindy asked, with a bit of trepidation in her voice.

Slim pulled off his hat and scratched the top of his head. "Well, now, ma'am, I reckon they's gonna fight."

"And what happens if he loses?" Colleen asked.

Slim put his hat back on his head, then looked directly at the two women and said, "Let's just hope he wins, otherwise we got ourselves a passel of trouble."

Clay and Blue Coat circled each other, each taking the others measure. Clay's foot tripped on a piece of something that momentarily threw him off balance and Blue Coat wasted no time lunging, slicing his knife towards Clay's midsection.

Clay saw what was about to happen and instead of trying to right himself he dropped to his shoulder and rolled over, coming back to his feet.

When Blue Coat's lunge missed, it threw him off balance and as he staggered by, Clay slashed out and cut Blue Coat on the upper part of his arm.

Blue Coat looked down and saw the trickle of blood running down his arm and turned to meet Clay, fire burning in his eyes. To let this white man beat him would be a disgrace he could not bear. Was he not, Blue Coat, a mighty Shawnee warrior that no white man could kill?

For close to twenty minutes, they parried and slashed at one another, each drawing blood several times. Both were getting tired and Clay decided to end this, once and for all.

Before Blue Coat had a chance to react, Clay rushed him and grabbed the hand with the knife, then put his foot behind Blue Coat's leg and drove his weight toward Blue Coat, tripping him. The big Indian landed on his back, surprise on his face when he felt the edge of Clay's knife against his throat.

To Clay's surprise, Blue Coat began to sing his death song.

Clay didn't want to kill this man, or any other man for that matter, Indian or white. "You can relax, I'm not gonna kill you – but I have won the fight and now we will part as men of honor. You will go back ta your people and I will go back ta mine. When we leave, there will be five head of cattle for you to take back ta your camp."

With that, Clay stood up and headed back toward his horse, praying this would be the end of it.

Blue Coat got to his feet, feeling humiliated. He had lost a hand-to-hand fight to a white man. He looked toward his braves and knew he could not go back if he did not kill this man. They would no longer look up to him - he would be dishonored.

Blue Coat let out a wild scream and lunged at Clay, who only had time to turn and block the down thrust of Blue Coat's knife and then, purely by reaction, drove his own knife into Blue Coat's stomach.

They stood there for what seemed a long time before Blue Coat slid off Clay's knife and dropped to the ground, singing his death song.

Clay hadn't wanted to kill this man, but he'd had no choice. After wiping his knife blade on the grass, he put on his shirt and gun belt. As he put on his hat, he looked at the braves still sitting on their horses and yelled, "He was a brave warrior and fought hard. You can be proud of him, but today was his day ta die."

Clay jammed his hat on his head and stepped aboard his horse. Before leaving, Clay looked at the Indians still sitting their ponies, and raised his arm in triumph.

When he rode into camp, he said, "Slim, when we leave, you and Riley cut out five head and leave them here."

Colleen looked at Clay and said. "Tis ah strange man you are, Clay Brentwood. But an honorable one I should say. Ya do battle with a savage that wants ta kill ya, then leave his people some of yer precious cattle."

"He was a brave warrior and I got lucky. They will take the cattle and be thankful. If we should pass this way again, I'm hopin' they will remember."

"You've been cut and need tendin'," Colleen said.

"Nothin' so serious that I can't wait til evenin' and we're sure they won't be comin' after us."

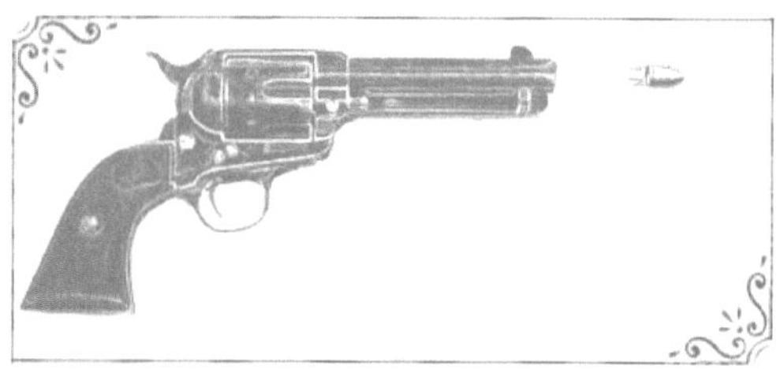

CHAPTER FIVE

-

On the sixteenth day of the drive, the sun was almost directly overhead and it was hot. Clay had just given the order to take a break for the noon meal when Bert came riding up, his eyes wild with excitement and mixed with fear, yelling, "Injuns!" then turned his horse and rode back in the direction he came from, pulling his rifle from its boot.

Clay looked toward where Bert had come from and sure enough, four Indians were riding in their direction, but they were in no particular hurry and weren't wearing war paint. Clay climbed aboard his horse and followed Bert.

Recognition came just as Bert raised his rifle and fired.

At the sound of Bert's rifle, all four Indians turned their horses and rode hell bent for leather out of rifle range, then turned and looked back toward Clay and the herd.

Clay raced the black stallion up to Bert and jerked the rifle out of his hands.

"What'ya doin' boss? They's Injuns! Savages! We gotta defend ourselves," he yelled.

"Not from these Indians," Clay said, sternly. "They're friendly and they work for me!"

Bert looked at Clay with genuine surprise on his face. "You funnin' me?" he asked. "I ain't never heered ah no friendly Injuns. Fella back home says they's all savages and need ta be wiped off the face of the earth."

"Your friend is an idiot," Clay said, looking in the direction of the four Indians, then turned and looked back at the other men. "Hold your fire. They're friendly."

Clay raised his arm, letting the four Indians know everything was all right and motioned for them to come on in, then turned back to Bert. "These men are Comanche. They're friends of mine and they work for me, and I'll bet they have more education than you do," he said. "See that big one on the paint? His name is Running Coyote. He's a sub- chief of his tribe and he can read, write and speak four languages. The heavy set one on his left is Brave Eagle, and knows more about treatin' sick animals than any of us. The one on the other side is He Who Bites.

He's one of the best trackers and hunters in this part of the world. And the last one, the one bringing up the rear, is called, He Who Sleeps A Lot, and is the best horse wrangler I've ever seen. He breaks and trains horses so good a child can ride'm, or, you can work'm all day and half the night. They say he can actually talk ta horses and they understand what he says. His other name is, Horse Talker."

Bert shook his head and said, "Well now, don't thet jest cock yer pistol. I ain't never heered the like."

"And you'd better learn to get along with'm because Running Coyote is ramrod on the ranch when I'm not around."

By now, Bert's eyes were wide with wonderment. "Me, workin' fer an Injun? Wul, I'll be hog-swoggled. Ain't nobody back home gonna believe thet."

When they rode up and stopped, Running Coyote looked at Bert and said, "This is one time I'm glad you are a poor shot, white man."

Bert hung his head and muttered, "I'm real sorry about that, didn't know you was friends of the boss and one of us."

During the noon meal, Clay introduced the four Indians to his wranglers and vice versa.

"Any of you who don't think you can work with these men," he said, indicating the four Comanche, "just say so now and you can draw your pay.

All six wranglers walked a short distance away and had a pow-wow, with Slim and Bert doing most of the talking.

When they came back, Slim walked up to Running Coyote and held out his hand. "I got no problem with you, friend, as long as I can keep what little hair I got."

That seemed to break the ice and before long, they were all talking about cattle, horses and ranching.

Clay asked Running Coyote and the rest of the Indians to come with him and meet the new cooks and house managers.

Both women were waiting next to the chuck wagon and when they walked up, Colleen reached up and straightened a strand of her hair and then wiped the dust from the front of her dress. They were the first Indians she'd ever seen up close and they were certainly a lot more dignified and handsome than she had expected, especially the tall one – there was something about the way he looked at her.

Her eyes got as wide as saucers when Running Coyote reached out and took her hand and lifted it to his lips, giving her hand a light kiss. "It is indeed my pleasure to meet you and I'm sure we'll get along fine."

"Oh my," Colleen said with a stammer. "I surely do hope so," she finally squeaked out, feeling her cheeks flush. "And this is my daughter, Cindy," she said when she finally found her voice, again.

Running Coyote reached out and took Cindy's hand and also gave it a light kiss. "You are as beautiful as your mother," he said with a smile that made both women blush.

"Oh, I'll need ta be keepin' an eye on this one," Colleen said to Clay, straightening her hair again. "These aren't the savages ya read about in them dime novels, no sir, not by ah long shot."

Inside, Clay was laughing and feeling very relieved. A large problem had been solved – how to introduce his red skinned friends to the others without there being hostilities. He could now think about heading for Dallas. Running Coyote and Slim could take over the herd, and He Who Bites could lead the way to the ranch.

During the afternoon drive, Clay rode up next to Running Coyote and asked, "How did you come to know where we'd be, and why did you come lookin' for us?"

Running Coyote smiled and said, "The Comanche knows many things, like the fact that you would be needing some extra help, and to let you know there is a man who follows us."

With that he raced off chasing a stray.

Clay searched the horizon behind them and saw no one. But if Running Coyote said there was a man back there, you could take it to the bank, there was one back there.

The following day, coming up on noontime, a lone rider rode toward them from the east and Clay rode out to meet him. The sun was shining brightly. It was unusually warm and Clay felt sweat run down his backbone as he reached up and wiped sweat from his forehead and out of his eyes.

The man rode straight up in the saddle, like a man with confidence. When they got closer, Clay saw the reflection off a spot on the rider's chest and figured he must be a lawman.

Sure enough, when they stopped a few feet apart, the man introduced himself as the sheriff from Enid, Oklahoma.

"Had any strangers join your drive lately? Or maybe see a rider pass by in a hurry like? I've been following some tracks off and on for ah couple of weeks now. Just behind me a ways, maybe a couple of miles," he said pointing back toward the hills, "the tracks disappeared in the rocks. Saw your drive and thought I might make an inquiry.

Clay said, "No," but told him he was welcome to ride in and check out the men he had. Clay went on to explain that he was a Texas Ranger and the men in his employ, except for the four Comanche Indians, had been with him for the past several weeks. "Hired'm up in Wichita ta drive my herd back down ta my ranch in Texas – which lies a few miles west of Seymour. The Comanche have been with me for some time."

Clay invited the sheriff to stay for lunch and when they were settled, Clay asked, "What does this fella look like and what did he do?" The other men had crowded around, wanting to hear why a sheriff would be so intent to keep looking for somebody, several weeks after whatever happened.

"That's part of the problem," the sheriff said. "I'm only guessin' that it's ah man, and I don't have a clue as to what he looks like, but what he done was mighty vile and I want to see him brought to justice.

"We had us a man and his wife move into the territory ah couple of years ago, Alfred and Pearl Carpenter – hard workin' farmers and real nice folks. I make the rounds of people not too far from town from time to time, just to keep on top of things...

Heard she was in the family way and decided I'd drop by and see if they needed anything. That was close ta two weeks ago. I rode by their place - got there about noon. My gawd, it was awful!"

The sheriff stopped and took a deep breath. What he had to say was difficult, but after a moment, he went on. "When I got there, I saw the place had been partly burned, house, barn, smokehouse, and what I found inside the house turned my stomach… Mister Carpenter's stomach had been sliced open and his entrails were pulled out of his body and his throat had been cut."

"Oh my god!" Colleen exclaimed.

The sheriff looked up and said, "And that ain't the worst of it, ma'am. You might not want ta hear this next part."

Colleen had a hard time believing things could get worse, but she said, "I'm not so squeamish as all of that, mister sheriff man. Continue, sir. I want to know what I'd be up against if I should ever meet this person."

"Yes ma'am," the sheriff said, then turned back toward Clay and the rest of the men. "It was obvious that Pearl had been raped, then had her stomach sliced open and the baby had been dragged from her body and was lying on the floor next to her. Whoever this vile person was, cut her throat too. I buried 'em and made a couple of markers for the graves. Got no way of knowin' if they got people somewhere or how to contact anybody with ever'thing burnt up in the fire like it was," he said, shaking his head.

After taking a sip of his coffee, he said, "Can't understand how somebody could do that; not to such nice folks as the Carpenters. I found a set of tracks leading away from the farm that I knew didn't belong to their stock. Each shoe had a small x near the back edge. I've been goin' out from time ta time, hoping he might still be in the vicinity. Didn't find anything until I spotted some old tracks yesterday and followed'm up into the hills. By now, I'm so far out of my jurisdiction that my badge wouldn't be much use, but I truly did want to catch up to him."

The sheriff took a deep breath, then said, "I'm pretty much a peaceful man, but in the mood I've been in, it's probably a good thing I didn't come onto whoever it was."

The sheriff looked at Running Coyote and the others and said, "No offense, but I know Indians are known to torture their enemies before killin'm, but this wasn't like no Indian that I ever heard of. But, no matter whoever he is, I hope somebody catches him before he finds any more victims."

"No offense taken, Sheriff," Running Coyote said. "But I can assure you, if we catch this person, I will make it my personal responsibility to make him suffer long and hard before he dies, assuming it was a man who did this."

"Seems ta me it had ta be ah male, because of the rape and all."

Everyone looked at each other and nodded their heads.

While the sheriff finished eating, Riley took it upon himself to feed and water the sheriff's horse and give him a bit of a rubdown.

It was very quiet around the camp as they stood watching the sheriff head back toward Enid.

Finally, Clay said, "We need to put a few more miles on those beeves before the sun goes down. Let's move'm out."

Clay's last night before heading for Dallas was peaceful. As the nightriders circled the herd, Cindy lulled the cows to sleep with a couple of her songs from home. There was something about an Irish lullaby that the cattle seemed to like. She sang, the lament for Owen Roe, then, Girl I Left Behind and last, Patrick Sheehan. By then, it was getting late and the cattle were bedded down and quiet.

Earlier, Clay told them about having to go to Dallas to escort some owlhoot to the prison up in Canon City, Colorado.

"I ain't real sure how long I'll be gone, but Running Coyote and Slim know what needs ta be done before cold weather sets in. I'm sure you'll get along just fine til I get back."

Louis L'Croix, a Cajun out of Louisiana of medium height and weight, but a man who knew his way around a herd, tipped his hat back and asked, "What about pay and time off? Is there ah town close by?"

Clay grinned. He knew that after working hard and putting in long days, a fella needed a little time to himself once in a while. "Running Coyote has instructions to pay all of you at the end of each month, and two or three of you at a time will get time off, depending on how things are going. Seymour is about half a day's ride to the east and you'll each get time to go into town."

The men nodded their heads and started muttering amongst themselves.

Clay raised his hand. He wanted to make one thing very clear. "There's one thing each of you need to remember. Don't go in there raisin' hell and expect me ta bail you out. Enjoy yourselves, but keep your noses clean, if you know what I mean.

Running Coyote and Slim have instructions ta fire anybody who doesn't follow the rules. We've got ta do business with those folks and we don't want'm mad at us."

The following morning as Clay was saddling the black stallion, Colleen walked up to him and said, "Don'tcha be worryin' none. I'll help keep'm in line or they'll not be sittin' down ta my table, ya can bet yer last shillin' on that."

Clay looked at her and said, "Of that I have no doubt. Just don't be too hard on 'em, they're mostly still young and still not dry behind the ears."

"Well, just so ya know, we'll be lookin' ta see ya come ridin' back," she said as she stuffed a package filled with food into one of his saddlebags.

As Clay stepped into the stirrup and swung his leg over the saddle, he said, "That's good to know. And I'll be lookin' forward ta comin' home."

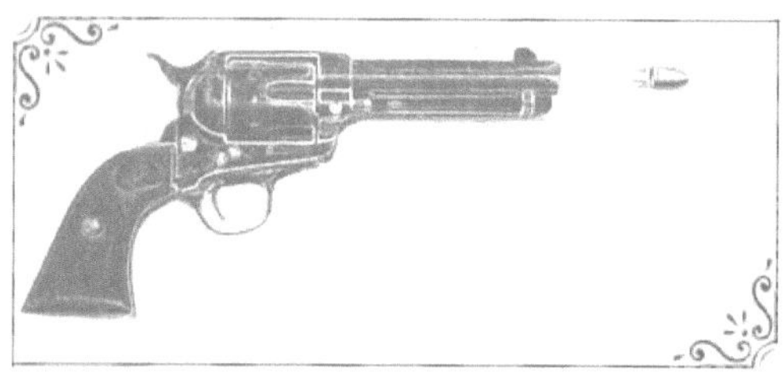

CHAPTER SIX

-

The sun was high and the weather was humid when Clay reached Enid. The first thing he did was check with the sheriff to see if he'd caught the person who'd murdered the Carpenters.

"He got away clean as a whistle." the sheriff said with a sigh. "After I left you folks, I got lucky and picked up his track again. Followed it to a ranch about twenty miles south and west. Farmer's wife had been raped and her throat was cut. And the husband had been stabbed a good ten times. I found the horse with the marked shoes running loose. He apparently took one of the farmer's horses but it had no distinguishing marks. Followed a track leading away from the farm, then I lost him when he mixed in with other tracks on the road."

"Too bad," Clay said. "Any other clues?"

"Now that's the thing. I found a set of footprints in the corral that could have come from a small man or maybe a woman, that didn't fit either one of the dead people, but it did fit with the horse tracks I'd been followin'. You know, the heavier the rider the deeper the tracks, and all his tracks were like those of somebody small.

Enid had a laundry and bath and Clay took advantage of both, then had supper at the hotel. Half way through his supper, Clay sat back and stared at his plate. The food was fair, but nothing to compare with Colleen McIntyre's cooking.

After buying a ticket for the train to Dallas, leaving first thing in the morning, Clay felt restless and went to the saloon for a drink before going to bed.

The saloon was typical, a long bar with a foot rail and spittoons ever ten feet or so. There were an even dozen tables where men sat and drank or played cards. At the back of the room there was a poker game going on. There were three men who looked like cowhands and what Clay sized up to be a card shark dressed in a brown gabardine suit and a derby hat. His skin was pale like he rarely saw the light of day and his hands dealt the cards like they were a part of him. He was good; very good, but Clay saw him cut and slide cards as he dealt.

Clay walked up and asked, "Got room for one more?"

"Sure, if you're lookin' ta give yer money away," one of the cowboys said, pointing at the stack of money in front of the man with the derby hat.

Clay won the first hand with two pair and knew he was being set up; then lost the next two hands. On the fourth hand, the card shark dealt him three tens and a pair of kings. Clay studied the man, trying to understand his method of setting his dupes up. Giving him a winning hand to begin with, then seeing that he lost a couple of hands, and then giving him a hand that would normally win, like the one he'd just been dealt.

The cowboy on the dealer's left called and raised a dollar. The next man folded and the man next to Clay called. It was up to Clay to call or raise.

The card shark had a slight smirk on his face and Clay knew this was the set up, so he called and raised ten dollars. Everyone else folded except the card shark, who called Clay's bet and raised fifty dollars.

"That's a fair-sized raise," Clay said, lighting a cigar and blowing a smoke ring. "You must have drawn a damn good hand, or you're bluffin'. Which is it?

"Cost you fifty dollars to find out, cowboy," the card shark said with a grin.

Clay sat for a moment, sipping on the beer the waitress had brought him, then counted out fifty dollars and tossed it into the pot. Then to everyone's surprise, Clay counted out more money and raised, one hundred dollars.

Clay thought the card shark was going to have a coronary right there.

"Well now, cowboy, it looks like you're the one who drew a damn good hand or are you bluffing?"

Clay smiled and nodded his head. "It's gonna cost you a hundred dollars to find out, city boy."

By now, the card shark thought he had Clay right where he wanted him. "There's still one more card to draw and another chance to raise, how much you willing to risk, cowboy?"

Clay drew on his cigar, then snubbed out the butt in the large ashtray sitting between him and the cowboy on his right. "You're in the driver's seat and it's your bet. How much are you willing to lose?"

The card shark leaned his head back and let out a long, loud rolling laugh, and when he finally stopped, he wiped his eyes and said, "I'll say one thing for you, you got gall, but the time for bluffing is over." And with that he dealt the final card and then pushed all his chips into the middle of the table. "I'm all in, cowboy. Now put up or shut up."

After counting the man's bet, which came to four hundred and twenty dollars, Clay knew what he was gonna do.

During the game, Clay had seen the sheriff come in. He waved to him, and when he came over, Clay asked if he would watch his hand while he went to get enough money to call the man's bet.

"Be happy to, but it'll cost ya ah beer."

The young card slick started to protest but Clay assured him he wouldn't be gone more than five minutes.

On the way out, he ordered a beer for the sheriff.

Then, true to his word, less than five minutes later he came back into the saloon with a fist full of money. He'd gone out into the alley and taken the money from a money belt he wore under his shirt, but hadn't wanted to show in the saloon. That would for sure attract attention and maybe even get him a bullet in the back when he left.

Clay took his seat and dropped the money on the table, then looked at the young card slick and said, "There's the call, now let's see what you're so proud of."

The card shark grinned and turned up four nines. "Four nines, which beats your full house, cowboy." And with that, he reached for the pot, but Clay reached out and stayed his hand.

"What makes you think I have a full house?"

The look on the young man's face told Clay all he needed to know.

Trying to recover from his mistake, he said, "Well, ahh, what else could you have?"

Clay turned his cards over slowly, showing four tens. He'd drawn the fourth one on the last draw, which he knew had been an accident.

The look on the card shark's face went pale then turned to anger. "You cheated!" he yelled. "You couldn't have four tens, you shoulda had three tens and two kings… I"

He stopped in mid-sentence, knowing he'd said too much.

The card shark grabbed for his pistol but before he could pull it from the holster inside his coat, he was staring down the barrel of Clay's big forty-four.

As the sheriff relieved the man of his hideout gun, Clay said, "I think if you'll check his left arm, you'll find some holdout cards in a slider."

Sure enough, when the sheriff checked, it was just as Clay had said.

After the sheriff hauled the man away, Clay looked at each of the cowboys and asked, "How much did he take you for?"

The first cowboy said he'd lost a month's pay – thirty dollars, while the second cowboy counted what he had left and said he lost sixty-five dollars. The third cowboy said he'd lost forty-two dollars.

Clay counted out money, giving each one back what he'd lost. "Be careful who you play cards with in the future. If they're winnin' too often and too big, that might be a sign ta pull out."

The bartender set a beer on the counter and motioned to Clay. "On the house."

The following morning, Clay boarded the train for the trip to Dallas, wondering why he'd been picked to do an escort job? Escorting prisoners wasn't normal work for a ranger, so this must be something special.

"I must be the only one not on assignment," he told himself as he sat down in his seat and pulled his hat down over his eyes, thinking about how he'd go about getting the prisoner to Colorado. "A quick trip by train up to Denver, then down to Canon City, drop off the prisoner, and after that, straight down to the ranch. Nothing difficult about this assignment." He just hoped it satisfied his boss and he would be allowed to spend some time getting settled into his new home.

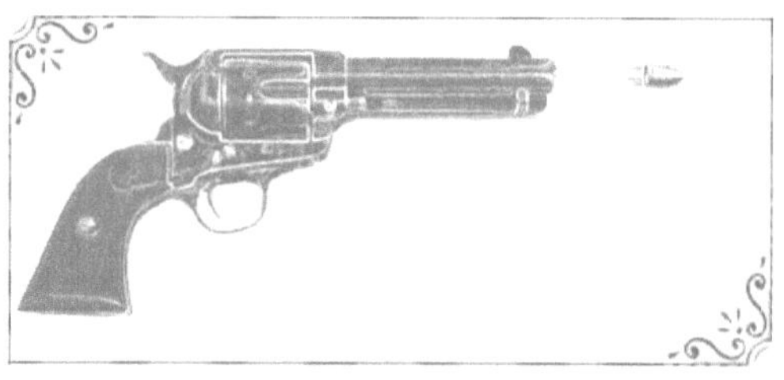

CHAPTER SEVEN

-

The train ride between Enid and Dallas, was for the most part, uneventful and downright boring until a woman of about thirty asked to share his table in the dining car. She wore a green dress that matched her eyes and showed off her figure, which was something to see. She had auburn hair and the front of her dress was cut so low that Clay was sure it caused many a man to swallow his Adams apple.

"Is this seat taken?" she'd asked.

Clay looked around and saw several empty tables, but before he could say anything, she sat down in the seat across from him.

"How does it happen that a good-looking man like you is sitting all by himself?" Before Clay could answer, she said, "My name is Amanda Coaltrain and I too, am all alone. Would you like some company?"

Clay looked at her and knew instantly that she was a working girl and more than likely, very good at her trade. He'd also heard about teams pulling the ole badger game aboard trains. If she had a partner they would clean him out once she got him into a compromising position.

He'd heard the stories about these women who took advantage of traveling salesmen or ranchers, or anyone they thought had money and he wanted no part of it. He would need to be careful. If she was working with a partner and Clay turned her down, she might start a ruckus, then her partner, who would conveniently be sitting nearby, would come to her rescue, claiming Clay had insulted her, which of course could be settled by a substantial payment of some kind. That's how the badger game worked.

He thought about showing her his Rangers badge to try to scare her away, but then he remembered something in one of the papers he'd been reading just before he came to the dining car… Why not, he thought to himself, it just might get rid of her without a fuss and he could have a bit of fun doing it.

Clay looked at her and smiled, then his right eye twitched. "I don't know how I got so lucky, but sure, I'd like to spend some time with you." Next, his neck jerked and his arm flew up like he'd been stuck with a needle and he let a dribble of saliva drip from his mouth.

The woman's eyes got wide and she scooted her chair back a little, ready to bolt if he got violent. "Are you alright?"

Clay let his head and neck convulse again as he twitched his right eye several times. "Oh, it's nothin' to worry about. Doctor back in Wichita said I have somethin' called, Dystonia. It's rare, they say. They're not sure yet if it's catchin' or not, but I don't think it is. I'm headed for Dallas ta see a doctor there who is supposed ta be a specialist for this condition. I'm just thankful I didn't throw up, which seems ta happen a lot when I start shakin'. My stomach gets all, queasy and…"

That was as far as he got before the woman stood up and without a word, turned and left the dining car.

Clay chuckled as the waiter walked up and stood watching the woman hurry out of the dining car like the law was after her. When she'd gone, he turned to Clay and said, "That shore be some woman. She comes in here ah lot. Mostly leaves with salesmen or ranchers. That shore was somethin' ta see. Is you one of them actors?"

"She is a temptation alright. But a man can wind up broke or dead because of a woman like her and I'm not inclined for either. And no, I'm not an actor, just thought I might have a little fun and I reckon it worked."

The waiter, an older black man with gray hair and tired eyes, looked down at Clay and nodded his head, then laid a menu in front of him.

Without picking the menu up, Clay asked, "What would you recommend?"

"Well sir, we got us a brand new meal called, spaghetti, and folks seems ta like it… It's ah noodle dish with tomato meat sauce on top."

"Spaghetti?"

"Yes sir. Let me get the cook, he be the one what makes it and knows more than I do."

Directly, a short, rotund man with long black hair and large, saucer like brown eyes came up to Clay's table and said, "I am Mario. Amos, the waiter, said you want to know what is spaghetti?"

"Well, I…"

"The spaghetti noodle was first invented by the Chinese and traveled around for many years before my people, the Italians, got a hold of it and perfected it. It is now…"

"All right, I'll give it a try," Clay said not wanting a history lesson on noodles.

His meal was served with bread that had a garlic taste to it, and instead of beer, the meal was served with red wine and Clay had to admit, it was good – not a thick steak like he was used to eating, but all in all, it was very tasty and he tipped, both, the waiter and the cook.

Clay lit a cigar and checked his pocket watch – six-thirty, and it was dark already. He figured the train would get into Dallas around nine. The ticket taker in Enid said it was no more than a thirteen to fourteen-hour trip.

He had just taken a sip of his wine when a brutish looking man in a cheap suit walked up and glared down at him. Clay could see the woman in the green dress standing a few feet back down the aisle.

The man had hands like small boulders and shoulders that looked like he could lift a horse without straining too hard. He had beady eyes and a nose that looked like it had been broken several times. He had the look of one of those maulers you see pictures of in those dime store novels.

"Something I can do for ya?" Clay queried.

"You insulted my sister and I want an apology and five hundred dollars," the oversized oaf said, placing his fists on his hips.

"That so? Well what if I say, no?"

The big oaf turned his head and looked at the woman, who nodded her head.

"Then I reckon I'm gonna half'ta rough you up a bit, then take all the money you got for making me mad. So, which is it gonna be, five hundred dollars or all yer money?"

"So, she didn't buy the rare disease thing, huh?"

The man looked at Clay like he was confused. "I don't know nuthin' bout no disease. I just want you ta apologize ta my sister and give her five hundred bucks."

Clay scooted his chair back and stood up. The man was at least a head taller and sixty pounds heavier. "Five hundred dollars is ah lot of money. What if I don't have that kind of money?"

Clay could see the other passengers sitting in silence, watching and waiting to see what was going to happen. He knew what they would do if they were in his boots – give the man the money, if they had it to give.

The man looked at Clay and said, "If you ain't got five hundred dollars, then I'm just gonna hafta take what cash you got and take the rest of it outta yer hide."

Clay reached into his shirt pocket and pulled out his badge. "You've pulled the badger game on the wrong man. I'm a Texas Ranger and you're both under arrest," Clay said.

The big oaf looked at the badge, and then at the woman who nodded her head, again, and without saying a word, the big oaf swung a right at Clay's head.

Clay wasn't looking for a fight, especially just after eating a large meal. The roundhouse was slow and Clay ducked under it and drove his fist into the man's gut. He heard a loud rush of air expelling from him as he staggered backward.

Stepping to the side and before the man could react; Clay grabbed him by the back of the neck and drove his face against the table. Other than bloodying his nose and mouth, it didn't seem Clay had hurt him much. The man might not be the brightest star in the sky, but he was tough, Clay thought as he watched the man shake it off.

The man straightened up and grinned. With blood running down the front of his shirt, he backhanded Clay with a right that lifted him off his feet and threw him backward, lights flashing off and on in his brain.

Clay landed hard and had a difficult time getting to his feet because his world kept spinning round and round. He doubted a mule could kick that hard.

Fortunately for Clay, the man was in no hurry and thought he had all the time in the world to work him over, because he waited for Clay to get to his feet before he waded in with fists swinging.

He hit Clay a blow on the left shoulder that felt like he'd been hit with a sledgehammer. His left arm went numb. He knew he couldn't take a hit like that to his other arm or he'd be nothing more than a punching bag for the woman's so called "brother".

Clay ducked under the next swing and drove his right fist into the man's kidney area, three times, and watched him stagger, but still didn't go down.

Damn, what do I have ta do ta put this big goon down? Clay thought to himself as he moved out of range of the man's huge fist.

They circled each other, looking for an opening, but neither willing to give up much.

Clay's breath was still labored when he took a hard blow to the ribs and gasped in pain. He moved out of range, again, but couldn't breathe without having excruciating pain. He knew he couldn't take much more of this, so he squared himself around in front of the man and grinned at him.

When Clay stood flat-footed right in front of him, grinning, the big man stopped and looked at Clay, wondering what he had up his sleeve.

Suddenly, Clay's head jerked upward and looked at the ceiling.

When the big goon looked upward to see what Clay was looking at, Clay kicked him between the legs.

The man's eyes got wide and he grabbed himself, but didn't go down.

This was no ordinary man. He should have been writhing on the floor, but instead, he got a look of hate on his face and charged Clay with both arms outstretched.

There was no place to run and Clay was in no condition to stand toe to toe with this big oaf, so he did the only thing he could think of. He ducked under the man's arms and as the man went past, he jerked his pistol out of his holster and slammed the butt down against the back of the man's head. His forward momentum drove him into the seat in front of him, where he smashed his head against the wall of the train car, then slumped to the floor.

With his left arm dangling and his ribcage screaming with pain, Clay turned toward the woman and saw her standing a short distance away, pointing a two-shot derringer at him.

"After what your goon put me through, you think that little popgun is gonna stop me?" Clay asked, walking toward her.

She got a confused look on her face and glanced down at the small pistol in her hand, which gave Clay just long enough to step up next to her and grab her wrist with his good hand.

Clay jerked her toward him just as the big oaf somehow got to his feet, bleeding from his nose and mouth, staggering around, trying to focus his eyes.

There was hatred in the woman's eyes as she screamed at Clay, "You, you..." as she pulled the trigger, hoping to shoot Clay.

The sound of the derringer filled the dining car and the big oaf got a strange look on his face and looked down at his chest. There was a small red spot in the middle of his shirt that was spurting blood. The big man sat down on the seat and looked up. "Why'd ya shoot me? I'm on yer side." And with that, he toppled over onto the floor, dead.

"See what you made me do!" she yelled.

Clay paid her no attention as he secured her to a seat and then took statements from several of the people in the dining car.

Clay hobbled to the bar to have a whiskey, which the bartender provided for free.

The bartender looked at Clay and said, "Looks like she picked on the wrong man this time."

"She's done this before, I take it," Clay said.

"Yes sir, several times that I know if. This is her territory, if you know what I mean."

"Why does the railroad put up with her if they know what she's doin'?" Clay asked.

"Not real sure about that," he said, shaking his head. "I don't stick my nose in where it doesn't belong. Safer that way."

Well she's taken her last train ride for a while if I have anything ta say about it." Clay said with a shake of his head.

When they got to Dallas, a man introduced himself as a railroad detective and said he would see that charges were brought against her for extortion and murder.

Clay gave him the statements he'd taken from the passengers, along with one of his own. The man thanked him, saying, "This should be enough to put her away for a long, long time. And don't worry about her partner, I'll see he gets taken care of."

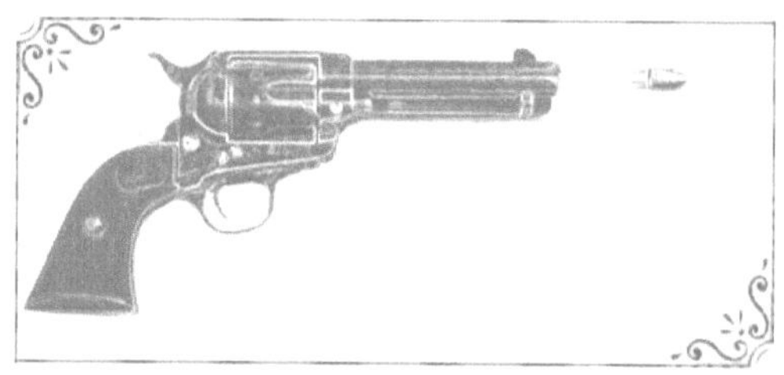

CHAPTER EIGHT

-

After waking up the man at the livery stable and boarding his horse, he got directions to the doctor's house.

There was a light on inside so he figured the doctor was still up as he made his way up to the front door and rapped lightly.

The woman who opened the door was slight of build and wore glasses. She was dressed in a plain dress and her gray hair was done up in a bun. She had a pleasant face, but she didn't seem to like being disturbed this late at night. She started to say something, then took a second look at Clay and ushered him into the house, calling out, "Horace, we have an injured man here."

The doctor was sitting in a stuffed chair, reading a book and smoking a pipe. He looked up at Clay and frowned. "Another barroom brawl, I suppose. What's the other one look like? Will he be along, too?"

Clay introduced himself and apologized for the lateness and then explained why he was so banged up.

The doctor stood up and said, "Follow me." Then to the woman, he said, "Mama, get some hot water and binding."

One of the bedrooms at the back of the house had been converted into an examination room. He instructed Clay to strip down to the waist so he could examine him.

Clay's left shoulder was black and blue, as well as his side. His right eye was swollen almost shut and his mouth had dried blood sticking to his lip and jaw.

"You're one of the lucky ones," the doctor said, wiping blood from Clay's face with a wet towel.

"Lucky ones?" Clay asked.

"Most of 'em get taken off the train dead with broken necks, or so badly beaten they're afraid to talk."

As the doctor bound Clay's ribs, Clay asked, "She been doin' that for some time, has she?"

The doctor's wife looked up at him and asked, "It's been going on for close to a year now, hasn't it Horace?"

The doctor looked at her and said, "About that, mama, about that."

"And nobody's done anythin' about it?" Clay asked, not understanding.

"Payoffs, young fella, payoffs. They're all in on it. By the time they bring them to me, the victim is either dead or in no shape to testify. They've got a story concocted about what happened and the sheriff can't get anyone to testify against her. They're all afraid of her."

"Well, she won't get away this time," Clay said. "I filed ah claim against her and turned her over to the railroad detective."

The doctor looked at Clay and asked, "Large man with a droopy moustache and a scar on his cheek?"

Clay thought for a moment then said, "Yes, that's him. Why, somethin' wrong?"

"Oh, he's a railroad detective all right, but he's also on her payroll. He's paid well to do exactly what he did. All you did was slow them down until she can pick up a new goon."

Clay paid the doctor and thanked him, then headed for the sheriff's office.

When Clay opened the door and stepped in, an old man with a bushy beard and small eyes, jumped up from behind the desk with a rifle in his hands.

Clay held up his hands and said, "Hold on deputy. I'm the Texas Ranger sent here ta escort your prisoner ta the prison up in Colorado."

The old man looked at Clay and asked, "You the only one they sent?"

"How many prisoners will I be escortin' ta Colorado?" Clay asked.

"Just the one, but I don't think I would try it without at least four men. He's ah mean'n," the deputy said.

"Maybe I should take a look at this desperado before I make up my mind," Clay said.

"Sure," the deputy said and grabbed a set of keys and unlocked the door leading back to the cells.

"That's him," the deputy said, pointing at a man sleeping under a blanket.

Clay called out, "Hey, you, wake up."

The blanket slid to the floor and a young man who could have passed for a Sunday school teacher, swung his legs over the side of the bed and sat up and stared at Clay.

At first, Clay couldn't believe the deputy knew what he was talking about until he looked the young man in the eyes and what he saw made chills run down his spine. His eyes were cold and blank lookin', like a dead man's eyes would be.

"I'm Texas Ranger, Clay Brentwood. Come mornin', you and me will be headin' ta Colorado. You try anything and they won't be needin' a rope ta hang ya cause I'll fill ya so full of lead there won't be rope strong enough ta hold ya."

The young man just smirked and lay back down, dragging the blanket back over his shoulders.

Back in the sheriff's office, the deputy said, "The sheriff should be here between seven and eight in the mornin', right after he has his breakfast down at Molly's."

"Reckon I'll see him in the mornin', then," Clay said and headed for the hotel.

On the way to the hotel, Clay heard the train whistle and looked in that direction and stopped in his tracks. The woman in the green dress was boarding the train before it picked up too much speed.

Clay shook his head. It was too late to try and catch the train. It would be gone before he could get down to the station. He would send a letter to his boss, informing him of what was going on and hoped he could do something about it.

Clay had a restless night; he couldn't get the look in the young man's eyes out of his mind. He may look innocent enough, but his eyes told a different story.

Clay got lucky and caught the sheriff in Molly's, having breakfast. The sheriff asked him to sit down. "There are some things you need to know about the man you'll be escorting to Colorado," he said with his mouth half full.

The sheriff finished eating and had just pushed his plate away when the waitress brought Clay his breakfast.

"You go ahead and eat and I'll talk if you don't mind," the sheriff said, lighting his pipe.

Clay observed the sheriff. He was an older man, probably around sixty and beginning to get wide around the girth. His hair was almost white and his eyes had a tired look to them, yet there was still a commanding strength about him. His gun rig looked like it had spent a lot of time hanging next to the sheriff's leg.

"I'd sure feel a mite more comfortable if they'd ah sent more than one of you."

Clay looked at the sheriff, but said nothing, as he cut into his steak.

"He's not just mean, he's plumb crazy and slicker than ah greased pig."

"What did he do?" Clay managed to ask between bites.

The sheriff blew smoke into the air, sighed and then said, "It's not just what he done, it's the way he did it."

Clay's mind went immediately to the sheriff back in Enid and the story he'd told. This couldn't be the same man, could it?

"His name is Joseph Agular, but he's also known as, Little Joe Agular," the sheriff said. "I've got wanted posters on him from six states. We just got lucky. My deputy was out makin' rounds – you know, keepin' an eye on things. When he went into the saloon, he noticed someone sittin' at a back table, playin' solitary. The man looked familiar but he didn't know from where, so, when he got back to the office, he looked through the wanted posters and sure enough, there he was. He came and got me and we went over to the saloon and took him into custody. Just pure luck."

"Did he give you any trouble?" Clay asked.

"Trouble? No. In fact, he laughed and said he wouldn't be in jail long. He even said when he got out, his next two victims would be us."

"Well, he sure don't lack confidence, does he," Clay said after a sip of coffee.

"He just sits and stares at us with those evil eyes and smirky grin. Gives ya the heebie – jeebies."

Clay finished his breakfast and pushed his plate back and lit a cigarillo. "You still haven't said what he did ta get himself wanted in six states."

"Six states is all that I know about, so far." The sheriff took a sip of coffee, then looked at Clay and said, "He's murdered six families that I know of, and like I said, it's not just what he did. As I understand it, all of them were gruesome. One case I know about, the one up in Colorado, they said he tied up the man, his wife and their two small boys – then raped the wife in front of 'em. After that, he poured kerosene on 'em and set the house on fire while they were still alive… He admitted it with a shrug of his shoulders and said he could hear'm screaming as he rode away, laughin'."

Clay thought again about the family in Enid.

"He had a recent wound in his shoulder and when I asked him about it, he said he was up in Oklahoma and happened onto this man and his wife in ah wagon, goin' west and she was ah real looker. Said he pulled his gun and tied up the man and was just about ta have his way with the woman, when the man somehow got loose and shot him in the shoulder before he could escape.

"I asked him how it come ta be patched up so good and he said he was close ta dead when he rode inta this farmer's place just outside of Enid. He said they patched him up and took good care of him and his horse.

"And here is the gruesome part, once he was on his feet again, he killed the man by stabbing him and cuttin' open his stomach and draggin' his entrails out of him, then raped the woman and when he was finished, he cut her stomach open and dragged the baby out of her."

"Yeah, I heard about that one from the sheriff up in Enid," Clay said, shaking his head.

Clay could only imagine what the man had done to his other victims in those other states, but if it was anything like what he'd just heard, he'd help put the noose around his neck.

"I'll be going down ta the telegraph office. I've got a couple of telegrams ta send off then I'll come down ta your office and make arrangements ta take him off your hands."

"Sure do wish there was at least two of you," the sheriff said, scooting his chair back.

"I'll check with my boss," Clay said, paying his bill.

Clay's first telegram was to the sheriff in Enid, telling him he was sure he had the man who had murdered the Carpenters and would be transporting him to Colorado to be executed, and that he would be coming through Enid on the train.

The second telegram went to his boss in Austin, telling him he'd arrived and was about to take his prisoner into custody. He also informed him of the sheriff's concerns about needing help.

A reply came back informing Clay there was no one available and the budget was tight right now and to do the best he could.

Back at the sheriff's office, both the sheriff and his deputy did everything they could to try and convince Clay that it was crazy to try and take this particular prisoner all the way to Colorado by himself.

Clay thanked them for their concern, but without telling them about the telegram from his boss, told them he didn't feel he would have any trouble. He'd decided to travel to Denver by train and then transport him in a prison wagon from Denver to Canon City.

The next train leaving for Denver wasn't until nine o'clock the next morning, giving Clay plenty of time to send a telegram to the warden in Canon City, informing him of an approximate time of arrival, give or take a day or two, trains being what they were and the disruptions made by both, outlaws and Indians who hated the iron horse that chased away the buffalo.

Clay made arrangements for the trip with the railroad people who would allow him to cuff the prisoner in a back seat. He'd wanted a car by itself, but the train was almost full and a seat at the back of the car was the best they could do.

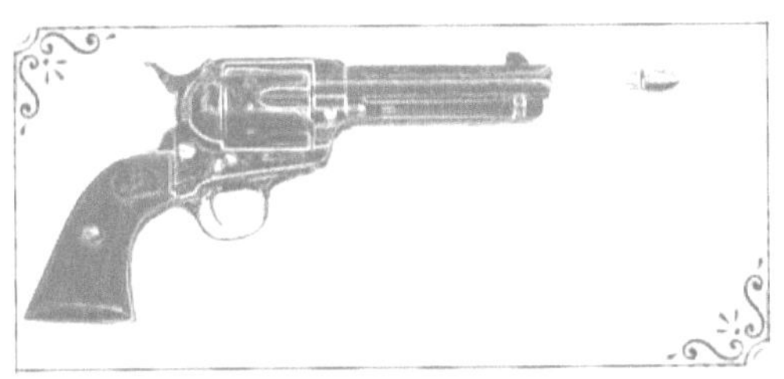

CHAPTER NINE

-

When the train pulled out of Dallas, Clay and his prisoner were sitting in the last two seats of the car. Joe was sitting on the inside seat next to the window. Clay would have liked to have had the window seat, but felt it would be harder for Joe to get away if he had to climb over him, which he wasn't about to let happen.

They had barely cleared the town limits when Joe Agular looked at Clay and said, "You should'a listened to that sheriff back there in Dallas."

Clay looked at him and got chills again. There was something about his eyes that bore right through a person. "You think so, do ya?"

"You think you've got things all figured out, don't you? Well, we'll see about that, mister Texas Ranger. I got me ah hunch you ain't gonna make it to Denver and I'll be on the loose again," Joe said with that evil smirk on his lips.

"It doesn't bother you ta do the things you've done?" Clay asked.

"Bother me? Why should it bother me? I just do what the voice tells me to do."

Clay turned his head and looked directly at Joe. "Voice? What voice?"

"Why, God, of course. He's the that one tells me what to do."

Clay studied the young man for a moment before saying anything. From the expression on the young man's face, he seemed to believe what he was saying, even though Clay had his doubts.

"God, not Satan?" Clay asked.

"God, Satan, what's the difference? The voice said he was God, and I don't question him. So, in essence, I'm doing the Lord's work… You know, getting rid of the impure. He said I'm one of his angels."

Clay felt anger rise inside him and before he let it take control of him, he said, "Shut up! Just shut up. I'm not fallin' for any of your flim-flam. Just set there and look out the window or you might not make it ta Denver."

Little Joe Agular's eyes got wide and he leaned his head back and laughed. It was not a laughable laugh, but a mocking, evil laugh that made chills run down Clay's spine.

When the train began to slow down, Clay cursed under his breath. The train would be stopping at every wide spot town along the line, giving Joe too many chances to pull something. But fortunately, everything went smoothly until the train pulled into Enid.

The sheriff was there to meet the train and wanted a look at the man who'd murdered the Carpenters.

"I could kill him right now and never have any regrets," the sheriff said, staring at Joe who looked back at him with a smirk on his face.

"I know," Clay said. "I pretty much feel the same way, but that would be too quick and easy for him. Personally, I'd like ta turn him over ta the Apaches. Now, those folks know how ta torture a man before they let him die."

"Excuse me," Joe said, looking up at the sheriff and Clay. "It's been a long ride and I'm needing to find an outhouse."

"Got one behind my office that should be safe enough," the sheriff said.

Since there would be an hour layover, Clay undid the restraints holding Joe to his seat and stepped back.

People watched as Joe, with shackles around his ankles, shuffled his way off the train and followed the sheriff.

Clay was about to go along with them when the conductor detained him. He seemed very distressed over having a murderer on his train.

"What if he's part of a gang and they try to rescue him?" the conductor asked.

"He's not part of a gang. I doubt any gang would put up with what he does," Clay said.

"But what if he gets loose on the train?" the conductor asked. "What happens to us?"

Clay looked at the man and saw real terror in the man's eyes. He was a small man, maybe five feet three or four and didn't weigh more than a hundred pounds. He wore thick glasses in front of eyes that were no more than slits. Beads of sweat were popping out on his forehead as the man shifted from foot to foot.

"If he does, I promise I'll shoot him before he can do anyone any harm," Clay said with a grin.

"But what if he overpowers…"

They both jumped when they heard two rapid gunshots.

Clay leaped from the train and ran for the rear of the jail.

The outhouse stood some twenty feet behind the jail and Clay saw the sheriff lying on the ground in front of it – blood running from his chest and Little Joe Agular nowhere to be seen.

The sheriff was still alive, but in bad shape. The bullet had penetrated his back and came out high on his right shoulder. Clay told the first man who came running around the jail to go for the doctor, and then knelt down next to the sheriff.

The sheriff was having a hard time breathing but managed to say, "Never… thought he would… jump me before… goin' to the john, but he did and I… wasn't ready. Shot me, then the chain… on his leg shackle."

"It's alright," Clay said. "The doc's on his way."

"Please… promise me… you won't let him get away."

"I promise," Clay said as the doctor ran up and dropped down on his knees.

When Clay stood up, a man in a suit who looked like a merchant, ran up and said, "The young man who shot the sheriff, jumped on the sheriff's horse and lit out going west like his tail was on fire."

Clay ran back to the train and unloaded the black stallion, then stopped by the livery stable and asked the hostler if the sheriff's horseshoes had any distinguishing marks to help him pick up the trail.

"Takes ah smart man ta think about somethin' like that," the old man said with a twinkle in his eyes. "Fact is, there is. Robin is the sheriff's town horse. He's got another one he boards here that he chases outlaws with cause Robin's got ah club foot and cain't run very far."

Clay looked at the man and asked, "A club foot?"

"That's right," the old man said, spitting a stream of tobacco juice into the dust. She was born with it – her right rear foot is some bigger than the other ones; always have ta make ah special, oversized shoe for that foot."

Clay thanked the hostler as he stepped into the stirrup and headed the black stallion, west out of town.

At the edge of town, Clay found the track he was looking for. It was headed toward the Cimarron River and maybe the town of Chester. By the long strides, Clay knew Little Joe was wasting no time, but according to the man at the livery stable, that wouldn't last long.

Clay gave the black stallion his head and let him run at a mile eating pace, but not so hard as to wear him down in case Joe found another horse.

Less than an hour later, Clay spotted Joe. He was still aboard the sheriff's horse, but the horse had slowed and was walking with a bad limp.

When Joe looked back over his shoulder and saw the ranger coming, he swung down and ran for the cover of the trees along the edge of the Cimarron River, not more than a couple hundred yards ahead.

Clay was still far enough away that it would be impossible for him to overtake Joe before he got to the trees. Once he got there, there would be a number of possibilities – one, he could be hidden behind any one of the large elm or walnut trees and would have a clear shot at Clay from a protected position. Two, he could try to make for the Cimarron River and maybe swim across, if he was a good swimmer, or, number three, he could stand his ground and take his chances at shooting it out.

When Clay got closer, he got his answer as a bullet whizzed past his head, barely missing his right ear.

Clay grabbed his rifle and swung down from the black stallion, yelling at him as he dove into a small ravine where he couldn't be seen.

The black stallion didn't like being shot at any more than Clay did and turned and ran back along the trail for a ways, before stopping to crop grass.

Not sure just where the shot had come from, Clay inched his way along the ravine to get out of the line of fire. More than likely the man had moved, but Clay couldn't take that chance.

Inside the line of trees, Little Joe Agular watched as the ranger dove from sight and saw his horse run back towards town. He checked the sheriff's pistol and realized he had only three shots left. After looking across the land in front of him and seeing nothing, he moved back into the trees and headed for the river.

The ravine ran down to the river's edge and when Clay got there he saw Joe emerge from the trees and start wading across the river.

Clay let him get about waist deep before he fired the first shot, splashing water up just in front of Joe.

Joe turned and fired before he saw a target, then turned and began trying to move as fast as he could into deeper water. He hadn't taken three steps when another bullet kicked up water just in front of him. He turned and saw the ranger and fired two quick shots in his direction, then threw the empty pistol into the river and dove under the water trying hard to swim against the current. But the current was too strong and when he ran out of breath and had to stand up, he was almost directly in front of the ranger.

"Be a lot less painful if you'd just give up without me having ta shoot you in the shoulder, or the leg," Clay said. "I could kill you right here and now and not lose any sleep over it, but that would be too easy. No, I think I'd rather shoot you in several places that would hurt like hell, but you'd still live ta see the hangman."

Little Joe Agular knew the ranger meant it, and he didn't like pain. Besides, if he were alive and healthy, another chance for him to escape might come up.

Clay walked Joe back up onto the higher ground and gave a whistle, then walked over to the sheriff's horse and checked her over. She was rested some by now and would be able to walk back to town as long as they went slow.

The black stallion raced up and stopped just in front of Clay and laid his chin over Clay's shoulder. "Good boy," Clay said, rubbing the horse's neck before taking a piece of sugar from his vest pocket and giving it to him.

Clay took up the reins of the sheriff's horse, then stepped aboard the big stallion before looking down at the young outlaw.

"Well, don't just stand there, start walkin'," Clay said.

"What?" Joe said with surprise. "It's several miles back to town. You don't expect me to walk all that way, do you?"

"Well, you just about rode the sheriff's horse into the ground, so, she's not an option. And I sure as hell ain't gonna let you ride up here next ta me. So, if you want ta get back in time for supper, you'd better start puttin' one foot in front of the other."

Little Joe folded his arms across his chest and glared at Clay.

Clay looked down at Joe and said, "Suit yourself," as he stepped down, bringing his lariat with him.

"What're you gonna do with that rope?" Joe asked, panic showing in his eyes.

"My first thought was ta hang ya from one of those tree limbs, yonder, but then I thought ta myself, that ain't part of my job, so I guess I'll just half'ta tie ya up ta one of them trees until I can get back with ah fresh horse."

"What?" Joe said, flabbergasted. "You can't do that. What about wolves, or Indians?"

"Reckon I'll just half'ta take that chance," Clay said, scratching the back of his neck. "If you've been eaten, or tortured ta death by the time I get back, well sir, I guess that'll be my hard luck. Guess I'd haf'ta bury what's left, if there is anythin' worth buryin'."

Joe sighed and looked at the eastern skyline and saw the outline of Enid and started walking. He had no doubt the ranger would leave him out here, where he would be at the mercy of any wild animals or Indians who happened to come by. He'd heard stories about how they treated whites, which was pretty much the way he treated his victims and he wanted none of that. Somehow, someway, he would get another chance and he would make the ranger pay. He would make the ranger suffer long and hard before he died. The voice would tell him what to do and how to do it.

Not a word was spoken all the way back to Enid, which suited Clay just fine. If the man opened his mouth, Clay might have to step down and use his fists on him. Clay wasn't prone to hating folks and didn't like feeling the way he did right now, but this young man had pushed him about as far as he could be pushed.

As they rode back toward Enid, Clay wondered what tragedy had befallen this young man to make him the way he was? It was sad when he thought about it. Clay also wondered about the voice he kept talking about. Clay had heard such stories, but mainly from preachers and such, but a voice that told a man how to torture folks didn't make any sense.

When they reached the sheriff's office around five that afternoon, Joe stumbled into the cell and fell onto the bunk too tired to care about eating and was asleep within minutes.

The good news was, the sheriff would be laid up for a week or so, but he would live.

Due to a report turned in by the frightened little conductor, the man running the railroad turned Clay down flat when he tried to continue his passage to Denver. Clay explained he'd already purchased their tickets back in Dallas, but the man shook his head. "I telegraphed the head office and they said to give your money back."

The clerk shoved a bundle of money in Clay's direction, "That man is nothing more than a cold-blooded killer and the railroad will not take the chance of him getting loose, again, and this time murdering some of the passengers."

Over supper at Molly's, Clay decided he had no other choice but to make the trip to Colorado by horseback.

Later, when he told the sheriff his new plan, the sheriff suggested Clay get someone to go along to help keep an eye on Joe.

"Canon City is more'n five hundred miles from here. That's ah twenty-day trip by horse, or more if the weather turns bad, and that's a lot of nights. You can't stay awake all that time," the sheriff stated matter of factly.

"I understand… and I appreciate your concern, but I'll be alright. He won't get away from me again, I can promise you that."

Along with thinking about the trip, Clay had been considering ways to prevent another escape, which if it happened again, he knew the first thing Joe would do would be to kill him without hesitation.

The next day, Clay bought three riding horses and a packhorse for the trip, knowing they would make better time if they changed horses every day at noontime. Even so, over the country they would be traveling, they wouldn't make more than twenty-five miles a day.

This would change his plan for getting back to the ranch, but it couldn't be helped. The railroad didn't want to take the chance of him escaping, again, and taking a stagecoach was out of the question – too many stops, if they would even take him, and not that much faster than going by horseback. No, the stagecoach was even chancier than the train.

The owner of the mercantile store gave Clay a questioning look when he made certain purchases, but said nothing. He'd heard all about the man the ranger would be taking to Canon City and grinned at the thought of what the ranger was going to do.

Clay was up early the following morning and sent a telegram to his boss in Austin, explaining the situation and what his new plan was. Next, he sent a telegram to Colleen McIntyre at the ranch, by way of the telegraph office in Seymour, explaining there was a change of plans and it would be close to two months before he could get back.

After breakfast, Clay went by to visit with the sheriff and explain his plan, which caused the sheriff to laugh.

"If you don't beat all," the sheriff said through his laughter. "If anybody can get him to Canon City by hisself, it's you, son," the sheriff said, still chuckling.

The sheriff laid some money on the table and said, send me a telegram when you get there. Let me know you made it."

Clay grinned. "I'll do that, sheriff, but you keep your money. This one will be on me."

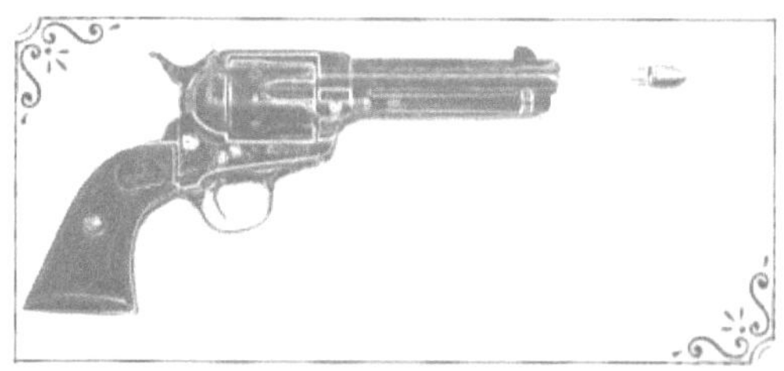

CHAPTER TEN

-

The sky was overcast the following morning when Clay and his prisoner left Enid. Clay decided they would cross the Cimarron River and then head northwest, staying between the Cimarron and the Canadian rivers up to the small town of Buffalo, Oklahoma.

He knew of a place just south of Buffalo where they could spend the night and the next day, pick up whatever supplies they might need on the way through town.

The first couple of days, Joe was in a sullen mood and said little other than when he had to take care of business. He was still upset from the surprise Clay had for him on the first night camp.

Instead of being tied to a tree where he might get loose, or in handcuffs that he might slip out of since his hands were so small, Clay sat him against a tree and not only bound him to the tree, but tied his legs together with a tether that allowed not much room to move around, and the other end to a tree some six feet away. Next, Clay tied Joe's hands to his sides so he couldn't untie himself. Then to make matters worse and to humiliate him, Clay tied a cowbell around Joe's neck, and smaller bells to other parts of his pants and coat, so that whenever Joe moved, he sounded like a reindeer at Christmas time.

"Are you that scared of me, Mister Texas Ranger?" Joe asked with a sarcastic grin.

"Ain't scared of you at all, Joe. I'm just ah particularly careful man. Never did like the thought of wakin' up dead."

"How am I supposed to get any sleep all trussed up like this?" Joe asked, glaring at Clay.

"Don't much care whether you sleep or not. Not much sleep at night will make you easier ta watch during the day."

During the day, they rode with Joe's horse walking on the left side of Clay's horse. Joe was on the opposite side of any guns, and where Clay could keep an eye on him. Joe's hands were tied behind his back, which made riding more difficult. Plus, there was a piece of rope tied around Joe's neck and anchored to Clay's saddle horn. Clay was taking no chances this time. If Joe tried to race off, he would hang hisself.

In the mornings, Clay stood guard with his rifle at the ready and let Joe go into the woods to do his business as long as he stayed in sight. The one time Joe's head disappeared, Clay put a bullet so close to Joe's head that he let out a yelp and never tried it again.

With their morning business finished, after securing Joe to a tree, Clay would put on coffee and prepare breakfast; most of the time they ate biscuits and bacon. At lunch they snacked on jerky, while the horses grazed. After the noon meal, they switched horses allowing for a mile-eating afternoon.

While everything was going smoothly, Clay knew he could never, for even one moment, relent his vigilance. Even though Joe seemed to be resigned to making the trip without giving him any more problems, he knew in his gut, Joe was scheming up some way to get loose.

The day before reaching Buffalo, a small town just below the Kansas border, Clay stopped for the day a few hours early, in a small grove of walnut trees.

"What's the matter, there's a town just up ahead where we could sleep in a bed for a change or are you plannin' ta keep me all to yourself durin' the whole trip?" Joe asked with a sneer.

Clay looked at the small-framed man and wondered what was going on inside his head.

"Don't plan on stoppin' at any towns longer than it takes ta pick up a few supplies. And ta make sure I don't have ta worry about you while I'm about it, you'll be locked in the local jail," Clay said with a smile.

"What if they ain't got no jail, Mister Ranger?" Joe asked, grinning right back at Clay.

Clay lit a cigarette and took a couple of puffs, like he was studying on the matter some. Finally, he looked at Joe and said, "Then I reckon you'll have ta stand outside and wait for me. Of course, you'll be shackled ta somethin' solid so you can't get loose and I might even pay somebody ta stand watch and yell if you try anythin'."

Joe glared at Clay; the meaning in his eyes said it all.

There was a small jail in Buffalo and the sheriff was a man in his early seventies who introduced himself as Carl Simpson. He was tall and skinny and his clothes looked way too big for him, but his eyes were clear and he wore a six gun with the holster tied down in a gunfighter's style. He moved with the grace of a man who knew who he was and what he was capable of doing.

After explaining the situation, Carl Simpson looked at Little Joe Agular and said, "Don't look like much ta me, but neither did Billy The Kid."

Clay didn't ask how he knew what Billy looked like. It was none of his business. He would be in town just long enough to get a few supplies, and by noon they would be in the Kansas territory.

According to the man at the mercantile store, it was thought the sheriff might have been on the owl hoot trail before coming to Buffalo and changing his name. The storekeeper was also quick to say that no matter what name he went by, or what he'd done before, he was a good sheriff and kept the riffraff out.

When Clay walked into the jail to collect his prisoner, the sheriff was sitting at his desk with his feet propped on it, drinking a cup of coffee. "Get yourself a cup, it's fresh," he said to Clay, nodding toward the pot sitting on top of a potbellied stove.

"How's our prisoner?" Clay asked after getting some coffee and sitting down opposite of the sheriff.

The sheriff chuckled, and then said, "Oh he started runnin' off at the mouth, tryin' ta act tough, but he's real quiet now."

Clay looked at the sheriff and asked, "Ya didn't shoot him, did ya?"

The sheriff shook his head and chuckled, "Naw. You'll see when we go back ta get him."

Clay's curiosity was piqued and he could hardly wait to see what the sheriff had done, but the sheriff was interested in hearing about the outside world. Apparently, they didn't get many strangers.

After half an hour, Clay looked at his watch and said he needed to get on the road and stood up, anxious to collect his prisoner and be on his way.

When they walked into the back area where the two cells were, Clay stopped dead in his tracks. He almost laughed, but caught himself. Joe was standing on a chair with his hands tied behind his back. There was a noose around his neck, looped over a beam in the ceiling with the end tied to the cell bars. He had a look of fear on his face, along with hatred in his eyes.

"Takes the rattle out of 'em real quick like," the sheriff said, grinning.

"Get me outta here!" Joe yelled. "That crazy ole man is trying to kill me!"

Out in front of the jail, when Clay had Joe secured to his saddle and he had mounted the black stallion, Clay put two fingers to his hat and looked at the sheriff. "You'll do ta ride the river with, Carl."

The old sheriff grinned and nodded his head, "You too, ranger, you too."

A cold wind was coming down from the north and it looked like it might rain as they rode north out of town.

The sheriff watched them until they were nearly out of sight, then headed for the barber shop.

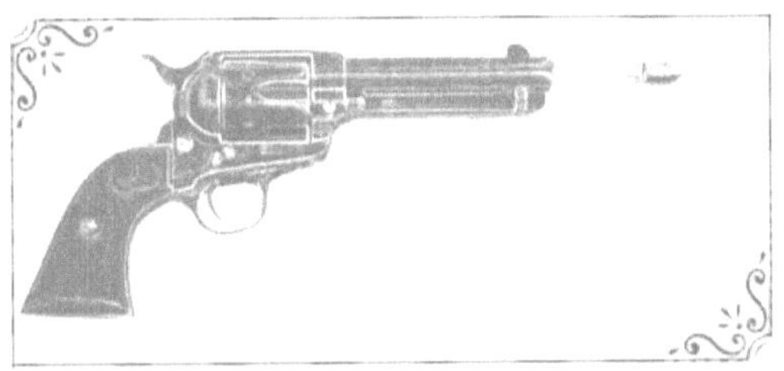

CHAPTER ELEVEN

-

After leaving Buffalo, Clay followed the Cimarron River up into Kansas. The days were long and trying. At one point, Clay woke up to the tingling of the bells attached to Joe's arms and saw him sawing at his ropes with a piece of thin rock he'd found and was using it like a knife blade.

On another occasion, just outside La Junta, Colorado, Clay was tired and had fallen into a deep sleep when something in his brain yelled danger. He opened his eyes just in time to see a rusty knife plunging toward him. He grabbed the wrist and yanked Joe's arm to the side, throwing him over his body.

Joe landed on his side and quick as a cat, he was on his feet, rushing toward Clay, who was still wrapped in his blanket and trying to get to his feet.

Clay couldn't believe Joe had gotten loose, but somehow, here he was. He had not only gotten loose, but had taken the bells off without making any noise, and now he was trying to kill him with a rusty knife he'd gotten somewhere.

Clay had just kicked off the blanket and was rolling over to get to his feet when he felt the rusty blade penetrate his left arm. The knife had been out in the weather for some time and cut more like a dull saw than a sharp knife.

Blocking out the pain, Clay came to his feet and looked into the eyes of the young killer and saw more hatred than he'd ever seen before. He reached for his pistol and realized it was laying under his saddle that he'd used for a pillow.

They circled each other in the moonlight, each looking for an opening.

Joe's voice was raspy. "You've played your last card, Ranger. Now it's my turn and when I'm finished with you, I'll roast what's left of your carcass over an open fire and eat my fill of you."

Clay had no doubt the young man meant every word he said. The point of the rusty knife still dripped his blood.

"Where'd you get the knife, little man?" Clay asked, taunting him by calling him little.

"Shut up! And never you mind. The voice said you'd try to use trickery, well it won't work."

Joe's eyes were glazed over and it was like he was actually listening to a voice as he nodded his head.

"Yes. Yes, that's what I'll do. I'll leave his entrails and what I don't eat, here for the wolves and other critters to feast on."

Clay knew he needed to do something and do it now while Joe was distracted by the voice.

Clay dropped to one knee and scooped up a handful of dirt and as he stood up, he yelled at the top of his lungs, tossing the dirt into Joe's wild looking eyes.

Joe screamed and slashed out back and forth with the knife, trying to clear his eyes with his other hand.

Clay quickly circled behind Joe and kicked him in the crotch.

Joe screamed even louder and dropped the knife as he grabbed himself and fell to his knees.

Clay picked up the knife, then went over and threw kindling on the embers from last night's fire, then put some water on to boil for coffee and to use to clean the cut on his arm.

Joe was still lying on the ground, moaning and holding himself when Clay dragged him over and tied him to a nearby tree.

Clay looked at the young killer and once again chills ran down his spine. He was evil through and through. "I don't know where you come from or what caused you ta be the way you are, but I feel sorry for you. You might have turned out ta be a useful human being instead of a maniac and menace ta society. It's sad, and I almost hate ta say it, but I'm gonna enjoy watchin' you hang."

Through gasps, Joe said, "You ain't got me there, yet, Ranger."

By the time they got to La Junta, Colorado, Clay's arm was infected from being cut with the rusty knife, even though he'd tried to keep it clean and bandaged.

It was still close to seventy miles on up to Pueblo, Colorado, then another forty up to Canon City. Clay knew he wouldn't make it if he didn't see a doctor.

As they rode down the dusty street leading into La Junta, Joe could see that Clay could hardly stay in the saddle. His head was slumped over and his breathing was ragged. He had been watching Clay get progressively worse and decided now would be a good time to make a break for it.

Joe's hands were small and it didn't take much to snake his hands out of the restraints on his wrists. Keeping his eyes on Clay, he slipped the noose over his head and gently let it drop down against the black stallion Clay was riding.

Joe knew he couldn't reach either of Clay's guns, but if he could get away he might have a chance, even if he couldn't kill the ranger, first. The voice in his head kept telling him he could do it and not to worry about the ranger, there would be another time if he didn't die from the knife wound.

"Well, maybe I can't kill you right now, ranger, but I can leave you with a lot of pain," Joe whispered to himself as he reached across and smashed the metal handcuff against Clay's swollen and infected arm.

Clay felt excruciating pain shoot through his arm and felt himself leaving the saddle. He tried to grab the saddle horn, but his arm wouldn't move and he was in no condition to do anything but fall. He hit the ground hard and then everything went black.

When Clay opened his eyes, his whole body hurt. His mouth was dry and he felt hot. His heart felt like it was beating so fast the rest of his body wouldn't be able to keep up with it.

Then suddenly, his jaw began to tighten and his body began to shake. He felt two pair of hands take hold of him. After a minute or so, the shaking stopped, and he was able to open his eyes.

Doctor Bryson Riggs, newly graduated from medical school in New York, had been in La Junta only a few months. He looked down at the man who had been brought into his office less than an hour ago. He shook his head, wondering if the man would live. He'd just finished cleaning and dressing the wound. It was badly swollen and full of pus. He drained it as best he could and cleaned it with hot water and added medicine to the opening. His wife, who was also his nurse, was handing him a clean bandage when the man's body began to shake. Together they had been able to keep him from falling off the table.

Clay felt exhausted. His body was racked with pain and when he opened his eyes again he looked into the face of an angel, or at least that's what he thought the pretty young woman looked like who was staring down at him. "Did I die and are you an angel?" Clay asked weakly.

The young woman smiled and said, "No, but thank you. I'm Melody, Doctor Riggs's wife and nurse."

"Doctor? I don't understand. Where's my prisoner? I have ta get up," Clay said as he tried to get off the table, but was too weak to get all the way up.

"Bryson!" Melody called out. "Bryson. Come quick!"

The young doctor rushed in and took Clay by the shoulders and gently pushed him back down onto the table. "Whoa there. You're in no condition to be moving around."

Clay's eyes had panic in them as he looked up and said, "I have ta get up! I have ta find my prisoner. He's dangerous."

Doctor Riggs smiled and said, "Don't worry about your prisoner, the marshal has him in custody. He's just in the other room, waiting to talk to you. Do you feel well enough to talk to him?"

Clay nodded his head and felt the doctor's hands release his shoulders. Clay watched him turn and leave.

A few moments later, a large man with a badge pinned to his vest walked into the room. He was not only tall, well over six feet, but muscular. He looked more like a prizefighter than a lawman. His nose looked like it had been broken several times and there were several scars on his face. His eyes were the only things that looked pleasant. They were steel blue with little flakes that sparkled.

"Glad ta see you're awake. Name's Crider Paulson. I'm the marshal here in La Junta. Doc says your ah sick man – tetanus, he called it. Says you got an infection from a knife wound and it's spread throughout your body. I don't mean ta sound too hard, but I need ta know about that man I got over in my jail, just in case you don't make it."

Clay was weak but happy to hear Joe had not gotten away. "How do you come ta have him in your jail?" Clay asked, ignoring the part about him not making it.

The marshal grinned. "You can thank Miguel Ramirez for that. He's ah vaquero who works on a ranch just south of town. Seems he was on his way into town for some supplies and came up on the scene just as your prisoner was escaping. When he started riding away, Miguel lassoed him and dragged him up to my office. I put him in a cell, then we went out and brought you to the doctor's office. You were close to takin' your last breath by the time we got you here. I noticed your Rangers badge and put two and two together and figured the young man in my jail is your prisoner. Now, just for the record, who is he and what's he done?"

Clay smiled at the thought of Joe being in the marshal's jail, and then passed out.

The marshal looked at the doctor and said, "Come get me when he wakes up."

Over the next three days Clay's body shook violently and his jaw locked up and he gritted his teeth so hard the doctor thought they might break. He was in and out of consciousness for short periods before his strong constitution took over and brought him back to the living.

Once again, when he opened his eyes, there was that angel. She smiled at him and said, "Hello, again. In case you don't remember, I'm your nurse, Melody. How do you feel?"

"I could never forget an angel," Clay said with a small grin. "If you've got any coffee, I'm thirsty enough ta drink ah whole pot and hungry enough ta eat half a beef," Clay said, feeling better than he had since he'd gotten sick out on the trail.

"Well, I think I can furnish the coffee, but we'll have to ask the doctor what you can eat."

While he sat propped up on his bed eating a bowl of soup, he gave the marshal the full account of Little Joe Agular.

He'd just finished his second bowl of soup and was sipping on his second cup of coffee when the doctor came into the room.

After a quick examination, the doctor looked at Clay and grinned for the first time since he had been brought to his office. "You must have the constitution of a mule," the doctor said, patting Clay on the shoulder. "How do you feel?"

"Better, now that I'm gettin' somethin' in my belly. I was feelin' powerful hungry. What's my prognosis, Doc? Am I gonna live? And if I am, when can I get outta here?"

"From the rusty knife we took off your prisoner, I'm guessing that's how you got what is called tetanus. It's an infection caused by bad bacteria. It's mean – causes spasms – starts in the jaw, then spreads throughout your entire system. Sometimes it gets so bad it causes other problems. You were lucky. A good many people die from it."

"So, I'm alright and I can go?" Clay asked, hopefully.

The doctor scratched his ear and made a face, then said, "Not yet. According to what I read in the medical journal, it takes several weeks to get back on your feet and even then, it might take several more months to get completely well, if at all. Some never do, I'm told."

Clay asked the marshal to send a telegram to the state penitentiary, letting them know he'd been delayed, but would be bringing the prisoner soon.

The marshal nodded and did as he was asked. He knew this man would not stay in the doctor's small hospital much longer. He also knew Clay would not allow anyone else to take his prisoner to the prison up in Canon City. The man had sand, he had to give him that.

Two days later, Clay woke up and got out of bed. He was weak, but by the time he'd gotten dressed, he was feeling much better. After some food, he would be ready to resume his mission. He knew it was still a good three days to Canon City, and he would have to take it easy, but even if it took him four days, he would get Joe there.

The doctor argued that Clay wasn't ready, but to no avail. Clay had made his mind up and there was no changing it.

After thanking the doctor and his wife, and paying his bill, Clay went and had a real breakfast with the marshal, telling him he would be leaving with his prisoner later that very morning.

"Been thinkin' some on that," the marshal said. "Kinda knew you wouldn't stay cooped up over to the docs, and would be anxious to be on your way. So, I said to myself, Crider, you ain't been on no vacation for six years now, and it's time you took some time off."

"Where you goin' with this story, Marshal? You got somethin' on your mind?"

"I'm goin' with ya. That's what's on my mind. Truth is, you ain't fit ta ride outta here and I got ah team of horses that need ah sight of exercisin'."

"No, no, no," Clay said, raising his hand. "He's my responsibility and mine alone. Just like this town is your responsibility. Besides, there ain't no fundin' for ah deputy."

"Now hold on ah darn minute. First, I ain't askin' for no money. And second, you got to admit, two of us watchin' him would be ah lot better than just one. And ridin' in ah wagon would be ah lot easier on you. Plus, if you should happen ta have another attack while you was out there on the trail, all alone with that critter. Hell, he'd kill ya for sure this time."

Clay had to admit; it would be better if he had some help. "Alright," Clay conceded, "but on one condition. I won't be needin' two of the horses if he's tied up in the wagon, so you half'ta accept them as payment."

An hour later they left town in the wagon with Clay's other horses trailing behind.

The trip to Canon City and the state penitentiary was uneventful and Clay had only one bad night of it. On the second day, he'd gotten the shakes so bad he couldn't control himself and he had to admit, he was glad the marshal was along.

Of course, Joe was hoping Clay would die.

When they drove through the gates of the prison, the warden came out to meet them, and after turning Joe over to the guards, he invited them into his office.

The warden was a small fastidious man with a pencil thin moustache and wire rimmed glasses. He was dressed in a tailored suit and was all business. He'd been worried when he heard Clay would be bringing Joe all by himself. The warden knew the people Joe had murdered and had been pacing the floor of his office, waiting for his arrival.

"If you don't mind," Clay said over a glass of the best tasting whiskey he could ever remember drinking, "After all that's happened, I'd kinda like ta stay for the hanging, if it's not gonna be too long from now."

"The man is well past his date to be hung, so there will be no delay. Will tomorrow be soon enough?" the warden asked, pouring a second drink all around.

The warden suggested they take the rest of the day and go see the large crevice not far from town. "They're calling it the Royal Gorge," he said. "The Arkansas River runs right down the middle of it. Even though it's really nothing more than a giant ditch, it really is something to see."

Since the hanging would take place first thing in the morning, the warden suggested they come back and spend the night in an empty cell, with the door open, of course.

Joe was full of bravo right up until the guards began to walk him up the steps to the gallows. When he saw the noose, his legs folded and he began to cry and say how sorry he was and begged the warden not to kill him. At the top, he beseeched his god and begged him to set him free and let him continue his mission.

The warden looked at Clay, who shook his head and said, "Don't you go believin' him, warden. He's play actin'."

When they started to put the sack over his head, Joe shook it off and looked at Clay with hatred, his whining gone by the wayside. He spit a gob of something putrid in his direction. "I'll see you in hell, Ranger," he yelled as the hangman placed the noose over his head.

When the body stopped jerking and twitching and they knew Joe was dead, the warden looked at Clay and Crider and said, "I've always hated executions, but in this case, I'll make an exception." And with that he turned and walked away.

Later, in Canon City, Clay said goodbye to the marshal who said he was going to take a few days and do some fishing on the way back.

Clay sent a telegram to his boss, Bill McDaniel in Austin.

PRISONER DELIVERED:

SENTENCE CARRIED OUT:

HEADING HOME:

Clay also sent a telegram to the sheriff in Enid, Oklahoma, telling him the same thing he'd written to his boss.

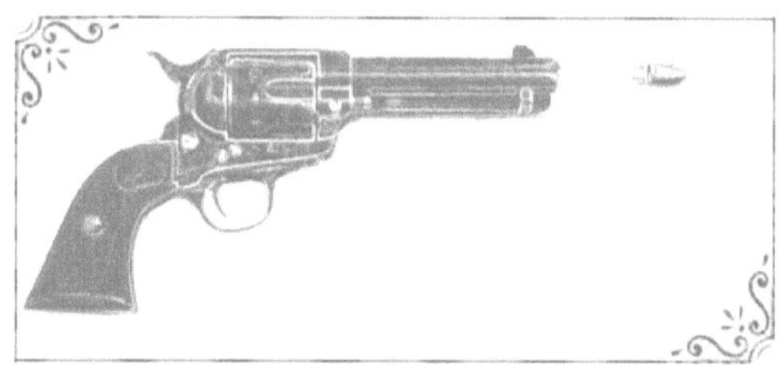

CHAPTER TWELVE

-

Around seven the next morning, Clay headed south out of Canon City, riding the black stallion and leading a buckskin mare, and a pack horse. The sun was above the eastern skyline and proving to be a warm day for this time of year. No one but the man at the hotel and the hostler acknowledged his leaving, which was fine with him.

Clay decided to take the shorter, more direct route on the way home. He had supplies for a few days, so he headed for Walsenburg, Colorado, then he would go on down to Trinidad, Colorado where he would make a decision whether to go over Raton Pass or veer off to the east and south and try to miss as much of the mountains as he could. This time of year could mean heavy snow in the higher elevations.

The next two days were spent riding at a leisurely pace. He was happy to be headed for home and sang as he rode along. He was fortunate to have a somewhat decent voice so the horses didn't seem to mind his caterwauling, much. He was anxious to get back to the ranch, but didn't want to push his horses; he had a long way to go. He stopped at noontime every day and had a bite, then changed horses. The weather was still holding but at this time of year, no one knew for how long.

Walsenburg wasn't much of a place. Mainly it was a coal mining town that had gotten famous because of a saloon owner by the name of Robert Ford. Ford had assassinated the famous outlaw, Jessie James, back in 1882, then came back to Walsenburg and ran the saloon before heading for the gold country in California.

Clay rode into town and stopped at the livery stable where he would leave the horses for the night. It was just as easy to sleep in a hotel when he could, rather than out on the cold ground.

Things being a mite slow this time of year, the old man who ran the livery was tickled pink to get Clay's business – three horses and paid in advance.

"Stayin' around for awhile?" the old man asked, hopefully.

"Sorry old timer, just passin' through. Be ridin' out come daybreak. Where's the best place ta eat and how's the hotel?" Clay asked.

"Don't reckon you got much choice about either since they's only one hotel and one restaurant, and they's both under the same roof."

Clay thanked the hostler and grabbed his saddlebags.

The whole town seemed to be covered with coal dust so the interior of the hotel was a nice surprise. The lobby looked clean. The lady behind the desk was of middle age and had a nice smile.

"Just one night, or will you be staying for a while?" she asked, turning the register around for Clay to sign.

"Just passin' through so I guess one night will do it. Although, I would like ah bath if one is available and somebody else's cooking besides my own if that's possible," Clay said with a grin as he signed his name and laid down a dollar for the room.

"We have both," she said with a mischievous look in her eyes. "You can call me, Sally and its two bits for each… the food and the bath, I mean."

Clay laid another dollar on the counter.

"Which do you want first, something to eat or a bath?" she asked looking at him with that mischievous look, again.

Clay swallowed. Was she coming onto him? She was attractive and mighty tempting if that was the case. She looked to be in her early thirties. She was tall and kind of willowy with bright blue eyes and even white teeth. Her clothes were clean and well made.

Clay figured her for a widow lady and her choices for male companionship here in Walsenburg probably didn't amount to much.

"If I get ah choice, I'd like ta have ah bath first. Don't mind ah little dirt, just ain't partial ta wearin' it," Clay said with a wide grin.

She handed Clay his key and a bath towel. "Room six, towards the back, right across from the room where the bathtub is. Shall we say, fifteen minutes?"

Clay smiled and put two fingers to his hat and headed down the hallway toward his room.

Just as he reached for the doorknob, he heard shots coming from out front.

Dropping his saddlebags on the floor, Clay turned and ran back down the hallway.

Sally was standing just inside the front door with her hands to her chest and when Clay ran into the lobby, she turned and said, "Don't go out there!"

"What's all the shootin' about?" Clay asked, looking toward where a man was hunkered down behind some wooden crates, firing a rifle at the sheriff's office.

"That's Rance Kane out there. He owns the Coal Dust mine just south of town. His brother got all tanked up the other night and shot a coal miner during a poker game. The sheriff arrested him and Rance told the sheriff to turn his brother loose or he would kill him. Apparently, the sheriff said no. Don't get involved. Rance is mean and would just as soon kill you, too."

"We'll see," Clay said, adjusting his pistol on his leg.

Clay walked out the door and turned toward the man crouched behind the crates. "Hey, you, Rance Kane! Put that gun down right now or suffer the consequences. The sheriff locked up your brother fair and square and he's gonna stand trial for what he did."

Rance was a huge man. He was dressed in a suit that wasn't quite big enough and the rifle he was carrying looked small in his big hand.

Rance looked at Clay and said, "Stay outta this cowboy or you'll get yourself buried right along with the sheriff."

Clay stopped some twenty feet from Rance and pulled his jacket open, revealing his badge. "I'm ah Texas Ranger and I'm orderin' you ta put that rifle down… now"

The big man looked at Clay and sneered. "You're not in Texas boy, you're in Colorado and that badge don't mean a hill of beans. Now get outta here before Texas gets one ranger, less."

"You heard what the ranger said, Rance. Your brother murdered a man in cold blood and he's gonna pay for it. Now put that rifle down and walk away. Ain't no need for the both of the Kane brothers to die."

The voice they heard was that of the sheriff, coming through the window of the office and it sounded old and tired.

"Better listen to him, Rance. He's givin' you good advice," Clay said with a stern look on his face.

There was anger on the big man's face and his mouth was contorted into a snarl as he turned and raised the rifle in Clay's direction.

Rance had the rifle halfway to his shoulder when the bullet struck it and knocked it from his hand. He couldn't believe anyone could be that fast and that accurate.

Rance finished coming to his feet and sized up the man standing in front of him. The man was powerful looking in a lean, rawboned sort of way, but he knew he outweighed him by at least fifty pounds and he was raised in a steel town in Pennsylvania and had been a knock down brawler since he was sixteen and had gone up against the best of them.

"Tell you what, Ranger. You got the nerve, you take that gun off and we'll meet out in the middle of the street, just you and me. You win, I leave and hire a mouth piece to see to my brother. I win, you suffer a beating in silence and back off."

Clay dropped his pistol back in its resting place and unbuckled the belt.

"No!" Sally's voice rang out through the growing darkness.

Clay turned and handed his gun rig to Sally. "He wins, shoot him," Clay said with a grin.

"What? No… You can't be serious. I've never…"

"Just funnin' ya," Clay said, taking off his coat and hat, laying it over Sally's arm.

"Be careful," she said. "He's already beaten two men to death, that I know of. He's mean, very mean and he likes beating on people."

"I'll keep that in mind," Clay said as he stepped into the street.

A little exercise before getting his brother out of jail would do him a world of good, Rance thought as he stripped off his jacket and rolled up his shirtsleeves.

Clay watched as Rance walked out into the middle of the street, and stood grinning like a kid who'd done some mischief. He was even bigger looking without his coat and his arms looked like tree trunks. He moved with the grace of a big cat, circling his prey, sizing him up before he struck.

Why couldn't I have just kept on ridin', Clay wondered. Or just gone on into my room and let the sheriff handle it. After all, this is his town.

Rance was stopped in the middle of the street, motioning for Clay to join him.

"Not gonna happen that way, big man," Clay whispered to himself. "I don't stand a chance toe ta toe with you and we both know it."

Without Clay knowing it, the next thirty minutes would be relived over and over for years to come by the people who lived in Walsenburg.

Along with Sally, most of the storeowners, the old man from the livery stable and the sheriff, all came out to see the fight, with most of them feeling sorry for the ranger who was half Rance's size.

Rance was a known quantity. Not only was he was big and mean, but he liked hurting people. There wasn't a person in town who wasn't afraid of him, including the sheriff.

"You don't have to do this, mister," the sheriff called out.

Clay took a quick glance over toward the sheriff's office and saw a squat, overweight man, who was bent over from a hard life and stoved up from rheumatism. He stood about as much chance of standing up to Rance as a leaf in a whirlwind.

Rance was standing in the middle of the street, waiting for him to do something. "Are we gonna fight or have ah stare down contest? You know you still have time ta walk away. Once I start, I ain't gonna quit til you're on the ground, all broken to pieces and can't get up."

Clay could see in the man's eyes that he meant what he said and suddenly got a knot in his stomach.

Clay looked over at the old sheriff and knew he couldn't just walk away. He'd committed himself and it wasn't in him to back down. He also knew the only way he was gonna best this man, if in fact he could, would be to out maneuver him, stay out of his powerful grip. If the man got a hold on him, he would crush him with his brute strength and leave him lying in the street.

"I was just givin' you a chance ta give up and leave peaceful like," Clay said with a grin.

"Well, I ain't about to give up to you, so I guess we'd best get on with what we came out here to do, if you got the stomach."

With that said, Rance moved with a speed Clay hadn't counted on and was within arm's reach in a flash and threw a right that caught Clay alongside the head, lifting him off the ground and throwing him a good five feet in the air.

Clay landed on his side and rolled over, trying to get the lights to stop flashing on and off in his brain. He'd just gotten to his knees when he felt Rance kick him in the side, lifting him off the ground, again.

Shaking his head and trying to keep from blacking out, Clay rolled over several times before coming to his feet. He couldn't take much more of this.

Rance saw the pain Clay was in and grinned. This cowboy wouldn't last long. And here he'd heard rangers were supposed to be tough. Well, if this one was any indication then their legend was nothing more than a myth. He turned to say something to the sheriff when he heard the ranger's voice.

"That all you got?" fat boy," Clay said, standing up. "They said you was mean. Hell, you hit like a girl and kick like a little boy."

With fire spitting from his eyes like daggers, Rance turned back to face the ranger. "I ain't even got started good, yet, little man. You want to see what I got, well, get ready for more pain than you've ever known."

And with that, he rushed toward Clay, ready to crush him with his fists, but Clay was ready this time and ducked under the big man's punch, driving his own right fist into Rance's kidney area.

Rance let out a small grunt, but didn't stagger. But when he turned around, his face ran into Clay's hard right fist.

Rance felt pain and saw blood running down onto his shirt. He blinked and looked for the ranger, but he had disappeared. Then he felt pain in his kidney area, again and turned around, only to stare at an empty street.

Clay was circling him like a prizefighter, waiting for an opening, then striking and moving again.

When Rance realized what the ranger was doing, he turned around slowly, looking for the ranger and found him standing there grinning like a schoolboy. Then before he could react, there was more pain; this time right in the center of his chest from a blow that felt like he'd been hit with a hammer. When Rance looked down, he met Clay's fist coming up to meet his chin.

Clay put his weight behind the punch and heard teeth break as the man's jaw slammed closed.

Not waiting for Rance to recover, Clay reached out and kicked him square on the knee, driving the leg in the wrong direction and heard the bone break.

Rance felt himself falling but couldn't do anything to stop it. For some reason, his leg wouldn't hold him upright. He'd heard the bone snap but the pain hadn't reached his brain yet. He was whipped and he knew it.

Rance couldn't understand how this had happened. As he fell, he could see the ranger standing there, dancing around on the balls of his feet and was shocked that this man half his size, this Texas Ranger, could best him.

Clay stepped back and watched as Rance landed face down in the street.

The townspeople stood frozen with shock. No one had expected the ranger to win a knockdown, drag out with Rance Kane. No one ever had, until now.

Clay had just walked over and strapped on his gun when Sally's eyes got wide and she screamed, "Look out, he's got a gun!"

Clay heard the derringer go off and felt a sting on his ear as the bullet went by and saw Rance pointing a small pistol at him for a second shot and reacted. Without conscious thought, Clay's hand flew to the gun on his hip and felt it buck in his hand.

The bullet took Rance in the middle of his forehead and he died before the second shot from his derringer could be fired.

For several moments, there was dead silence, then suddenly, the realization set in and the whole town gave a sigh of relief. The townsfolk crowded around Clay slapping him on the back. The reign of the Kane brothers was finally over. Bob Kane would be tried and hung for murder and Rance was dead.

The sheriff hobbled over and stuck out his gnarled, arthritic hand. "Thank you, Ranger. You've done me and this town a big favor."

Clay looked at the crowd of townspeople and said, pointing at the sheriff "This man is a good man, but he could use some help. If this was my town, I'd let him hire a deputy."

The old sheriff looked at Clay and said, "Thank you."

Clay turned and looked at Sally. "About that bath and somethin' ta eat."

Clay was soaking in a tub of hot water, letting it do its work on his sore ribs, when he heard the door open and looked up. Sally was standing there, barefoot from head to toe, with a bottle of beer in each hand.

She smiled as she stepped into the tub. "I'm thinking you might need a little refreshment and someone to wash your back."

Clay reached up and took one of the bottles of beer and after taking a long swig, he said, "It's been some time since I had my back washed."

CHAPTER THIRTEEN

-

The following morning, after a large breakfast paid for by the town, the ranger, Clay Brentwood, rode away from Walsenburg to cheers, and many of the people, yelling, "Thank you." His supply bags were loaded with things he would need for the trip, flower, sugar, coffee, beans, a side of bacon – along with fried chicken, a chocolate cake, and some fresh vegetables. They would have even given him a reward if he would have accepted it.

Clay rode the black stallion at a brisk pace south into the rugged land between him and Trinidad, Colorado with the packhorse finding it easy to keep pace. Both horses were bred to this kind of country and loved to be traveling.

It was only around forty miles to Trinidad, but that didn't mean the trip would be easy, even if he took two days.

While it wasn't heavy mountain range, it was hilly and barren of much growth. For the most part, it was rocky with a lot of up and down hills, which slowed down his progress. The air was dry and hot and there were few water holes, but lots of rattlesnakes and scorpions. He could've gone a little west and found spruce and pine trees galore, which would have given him more shade, but the going would be even rougher. He would be weaving between trees for the most part, fighting low branches, and riding on the side of a hill, which would be hard on the horses.

That night, he made camp just to the west of the trail he had been following. He found a spot in amongst some scrub pine on a small piece of flat rock jutting out from the hill, where he would be somewhat hidden by the trees. Behind him, there was grass for the horses, but no water. Fortunately, Clay had enough water to last them until they got to Trinidad.

After a good supper of cold, fried chicken, fresh vegetables and chocolate cake, Clay tried to read some, which was his custom to do before calling it a day. The prison warden up in Canon City had given him a book called, Moby Dick, by Herman Melville. The warden said it was a story about a man and a great white whale. Clay had never seen a whale, or the ocean, but the thought of it intrigued him. He'd seen pictures.

After a couple of chapters, he was hooked, so to speak, but his eyes wouldn't stay focused on the words. His mind kept going back to Little Joe Agular, wondering where he'd come from and what had pushed him to do the things he did? He'd heard of folks who claimed they heard voices, but Little Joe was the first one he'd ever met who did.

That night, he dreamed of being surrounded by men, women and children, all claiming to hear God talking to them and woke up with a start just as the sun was coming over the horizon.

It was cold. There was a thin layer of frost on everything and the hot coffee tasted good, along with the flapjacks and the rest of the fried chicken.

The sun was still low in the eastern sky when he started out. There were clouds racing across the sky, but so far, the wind was still high up, and Clay hoped it would stay that way.

Back down on flatter ground, Clay picked up a trail that showed a lot of use and he was able to make good time.

Clay heard Mexican music, along with laughter, several minutes before he entered the outskirts of the small town of Trinidad. It was coming onto late afternoon and the saloons were already beginning to fill up. The sun was below the top of the mountain to the west and the temperature was beginning to drop.

Lanterns were being lit, both inside the various places and out in front, making it easy to see as you walked along.

Clay stopped his horses and sat for a moment, looking at the people walking up and down the street. Most of them were Mexican, with a few white men dressed in miners' clothes. The Mexican men were dressed for the evening in their tight-fitting pants with flared bottoms and snug waistcoats. Their sombreros were wide and colorful.

He counted back and decided it was Saturday evening - a time for cutting loose.

The young women all looked beautiful in their bright colored flowing skirts and white blouses; their long black hair flowing down around their shoulders, making them even more enticing. They would stop and smile at him as he rode down the street.

After stabling his horses, he looked down the street and saw the Spanish and Mexican imprint on the town. He'd read somewhere that the town had been founded by the Spanish and Mexican explorers because of its proximity to the Santa Fe Trail. The town even boasted of having Bat Masterson as its marshal back in 1882.

Trinidad sat in between the hills just a little over twenty miles north and east of Raton, New Mexico, and was beginning to grow due to coal being found.

Clay stepped onto the wooden sidewalk and walked toward a sign that said, **ROOMS**.

Inside, a young Mexican man with slicked back hair and a pencil thin moustache looked at him and said in broken English. "Do you wish female companionship, Senor'?"

Clay looked to his right and saw several beautiful young Mexican women who looked at him with bright smiles and eyes promising pleasures beyond his wildest dreams.

Clay had heard of these kinds of hotels, but this was the first one he'd ever seen.

Clay smiled at the ladies, then turned to the young man. "Well… I reckon I'm lookin' for a regular hotel. Ya see, I've been on the trail for some time and I'm kinda tired and…"

"Down the street, two blocks, Senor'," the young man said, nodding his head in that direction.

Clay put two fingers to the brim of his hat and said, "Ladies," then turned and hurried out the door.

On the sidewalk, Clay saw several other signs that said, ROOMS, but not, hotel.

Two blocks down, Clay got a room on the second floor, facing the back, which he'd asked for to be away from as much of the noise as he could. Sleeping in a wild town such as this was a whole lot noisier than out on the trail.

After a quick bath and shave at the Chinaman's place, he headed for the restaurant next door to the hotel.

Clay liked Mexican food and was not disappointed, but during his meal, a brute of a man dressed in miner's clothes, grabbed the woman who had brought his food and jerked her down onto his lap. He was big and rough looking.

The waitress was a woman of about forty and definitely not one of the women of the night. She struggled to get loose. "Please, Senor', I am a married woman."

"That don't bother me none. I just want ta have ah little fun, then you can go on back to yer husband."

"Please, Senor', let me go. I am not that kind of woman."

Clay looked at the man standing in the doorway to the kitchen, who just stood there with a scared look on his face, along with the other people in the room, who also looked scared.

A man also dressed in miner's clothes, stood up and walked over to them and said, "You heard the lady, Joe. Let her go."

Still holding onto the waitress, the big miner stood up and smashed the smaller man in the face. "Stay outta this, Hank, or I'll hurt ya bad."

The woman was struggling to get free until he turned and slapped her across the face. "Like I said, you and me's gonna have ah little fun and by the time I get done with ya, you may not want ta go back to yer husband."

Clay had seen and heard enough. He stood up, walked over to the big miner, drew his pistol and clubbed him over the head with the butt.

The big miner released the waitress and slumped to the floor just as the marshal and his deputy came rushing in.

After a brief explanation, the marshal had the miner dragged over to the jail.

Clay sat down to finish his supper, to loud applause from the other patrons. The woman walked over and said, "Gracias, Senor'."

Clay, trying not to make anything out of it, smiled and said, "Think nothing of it. He was a big mouthed lout and deserved what he got."

The man from the kitchen approached Clay's table and said, "Muchas gracias, Senor'. You have done a great service this night and I would like for you to know there will be no charge for your meals as long as you are in town."

Clay looked up at the man and saw genuine gratitude in his eyes.

"Well, you're in luck, I'm just passin' through. I'll be ridin' on come mornin'."

The man smiled and said, "If you should ever come to Trinidad again, you will be welcome here and my offer will still stand." Clay knew there would be an argument if he tried to pay for his meal, so he tucked some money under his coffee cup before he left.

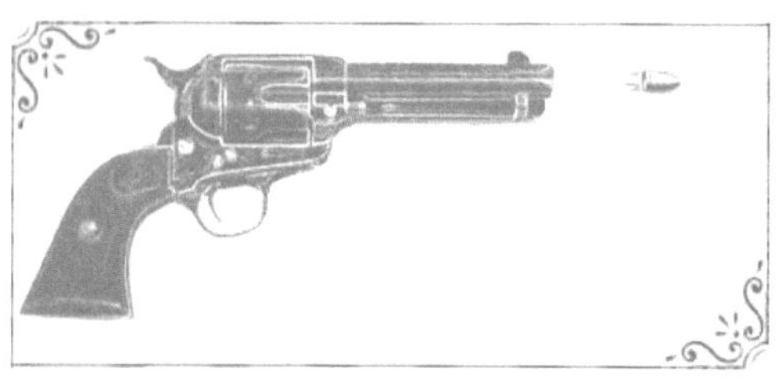

CHAPTER FOURTEEN

-

The following morning Clay was up before the sun, wanting to be on his way. He still had a lot of land to cover and bad weather could show up any time without warning.

When he opened the door, he saw a package laying in his path. He picked it up and stepped back inside the room.

It was a sheepskin coat, wool lined gloves and a cap that was also wool lined. Clay tried them on and everything fit like it had been made for him.

Well that settled it. He couldn't go back to that restaurant again. It would be far too embarrassing.

In fact, he sneaked out the back door and went down the backside of the buildings to the livery stable.

The man there smiled when he saw him and led Clay's two horses out, saddled, packed and ready to go. "Lopez, from the restaurant, said not to take your money."

Clay hung his head. "I didn't do anythin' but knock a man out, who was abusin' ah woman. That's all. Nothin' ta make this amount of fuss over."

"Oh, I beg the differ," the liveryman said. "That was Big Joe Babcock you knocked out. He's run roughshod over this town for six months now, and you're the first one to stand up to 'em. Even the marshal is afraid of 'em."

"What's gonna happen now?" Clay asked.

"Oh, the judge'll give him ah fine for disturbin' the peace and if he don't come lookin' for you, things'll go back like they was."

"You think he'll come lookin' for me?" Clay asked.

"Mor'n likely. He purty much holds ah grudge and he won't like what you did to him. My advice is for you ta lite ah shuck before he gets out."

Clay thought for a moment. He didn't want some tub o guts, like this Joe fella, sneaking up on him in the middle of the night.

"You hang onta my horses for a bit. I'll be back, shortly."

When Clay walked into the marshal's office, he looked up and made a frown. "What'er you doin' here? I was hopin' you'd be long gone by now."

"And have ta look over my shoulder from now ta doomsday, in case Joe Babcock is lyin' in wait for me? No sir. I'd rather get it settled now, once and for all. Can I see'm?" Clay asked, starting for the back of the jail where the cells were located.

"Your funeral," the marshal said, grabbing his key ring.

When Joe looked up and saw Clay, he jumped off his bed and walked over to the bars. "Well, well, look who's here, the cowardly little Texas Ranger who likes ta sneak up behind a man and hit'm in the head when he ain't lookin'. Why don't you come on in this here cell and we'll see how brave you are."

Clay looked at him and said, "Here's the deal. I whip you; you become as meek as a mouse. You don't bother anybody, you don't bad mouth anybody, and you don't cause any trouble whatsoever."

Joe looked at Clay and began to laugh out loud. Then after a good laugh, his eyes got hard and he said, "Since I ain't worried none bout that happenin', you got yerself ah deal. Now, here's my deal. When you get healed up from the beatin' I'm gonna give ya, you will pay me ah hundred dollars ah month so's I can live real comfortable like and you won't cause me no more trouble."

The marshal looked at Clay and said, "I hope you ain't plannin' on taken him up on that."

Clay nodded toward the cell door. "As a matter of fact, I am. Now, if you'll unlock the door."

Clay knew the man had run roughshod over ever'body in town with his tough talk, but Clay had a feeling he wasn't as tough as he bragged ta be. At least he hoped so. No, matter, he had to do this, and do it quick. He had to make Joe think twice before he thought about bracing him again.

"Step back," the marshal said to Joe, who grinned and walked to the back of the cell and turned around to face the door. "How's this, Marshal?"

Clay had no more than stepped inside the cell when he heard the key turn in the lock.

For several moments, they just stood there, looking at each other. Finally, Clay grinned and asked, "Well, are you just gonna stand there lookin' dumb and ugly or are you gonna show me what you got?"

Clay heard the roar come from somewhere deep inside Joe and watched as he ran toward him with his eyes flashing daggers and his big fist cocked and ready to end the fight with one blow.

Clay stood there, waiting until just the right moment, then ducked under the wild swing of Joe's fist, causing Joe to bring great damage to both, his fist and the cell bar when they connected.

Not waiting, Clay stepped behind Joe and grabbed him from behind and drove his head against the bars, three times, as hard as he could.

The big miner dropped to the floor of the cell like a rock and lay there, both eyes already swollen shut and his forehead turning black. Joe's right fist was almost twice its normal size and bleeding from the knuckles from slamming into the cell bar.

Clay walked over and picked up a bucket of water sitting close to the bed and dumped it over Joe's head.

The big miner shook his head and sat up, groaning, trying to see through his swollen eyes.

"You awake, Joe?" Clay asked.

"Yeah, I'm awake," Joe said turning his head toward where Clay's voice came from. "What'a you hit me with, ah sledge hammer?"

"You remember our deal?" Clay asked, paying no attention to Joe's question.

"Yeah, I remember," Joe said, holding his head.

"See that you do. And one more thing, you think on comin' after me, think twice cause the next time we meet, I won't be so easy on ya. I'll kill ya where ya stand and be done with it," Clay said in as stern a voice as he could muster, hoping the big man believed him.

By then, the marshal had unlocked the cell door. Clay walked out, down the hallway and out the front door without another word.

"I see you're still in one piece," the hostler said with a grin.

Clay took the reins of the black stallion, along with the lead rope to the packhorse, then stepped into the stirrup and swung his leg over the saddle and sat down. "You might want ta get Joe's horse ready. I expect he'll be leavin' town, soon."

The hostler stood scratching his head as Clay rode away, then turned and hotfooted it over to the marshal's office.

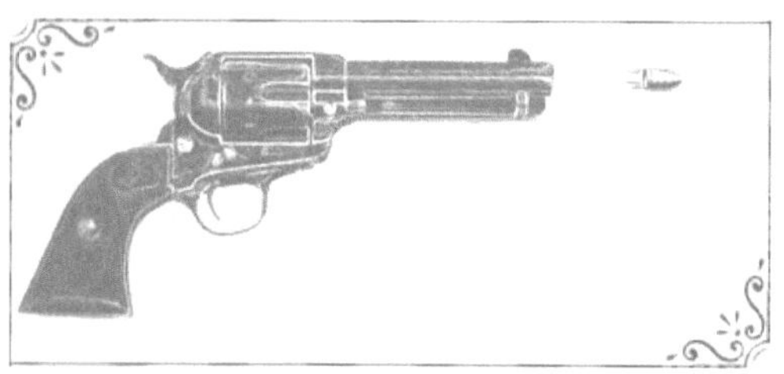

CHAPTER FIFTEEN

-

Clay left Trinidad heading south toward Raton pass, which he hoped wasn't closed by snow, yet. Looking toward the top of the pass he knew it was just under eight thousand feet and cut through the Sangre de Cristo Mountains. Back when it was first discovered, it was a narrow, very torturous trail; barely wide enough for a single wagon to crawl its way through. Since 1866, it had been widened quite a bit. Although this wasn't the only way across, from what he'd heard, this trail was the fastest and the easiest and that's what he wanted. He was chewing at the bit to get home and sleep in his new bed in his new house, and ride out among his cattle; and maybe chase down a wild horse or two.

He'd had enough rangering to last him a lifetime.

Clay chuckled when he thought about the name of the pass. He didn't speak Mexican or Spanish like a native, but he could get along and from what he'd heard, Raton meant, mouse, or, small rat. He guessed they named it that because in the beginning when the Spaniards came through, someone had said the pass was so narrow only a mouse or a rat could get through, and the name had stuck.

He'd only been on the trail for a few hours but could already feel the weather beginning to change. He could see snow on the top, but it didn't look heavy, yet, and he hoped it would stay that way until he was well over the top and headed for the panhandle.

The sky was turning gray and Clay worried some about it. Even though it was barely over twenty miles to the top, if a man got caught out here in a storm and nobody was around, his body might not be found until the spring when the snow melted. Snow up here got six to eight feet deep at times and a man or horse could disappear very quickly.

Around noon, Clay stopped and gave his horses a bit of grain and let them drink from a small pool of water that seeped out from a crack in the mountain. Clay looked around and was always amazed at how spruce and pine trees could grow out of what looked to be bare rock, but grow they did.

The sky was looking worse by the minute and Clay decided he would press on. He'd just put a foot in the stirrup when the first raindrops began to fall. Clay stepped back down and quickly donned his slicker and grabbed a few pieces of jerky from his saddlebag, then rode on up the mountain

By the time he'd gone a mile, the rain was coming down heavier and making the trail a rivulet of water, all heading down hill.

Clay looked for a place to get off the trail and up under the trees, but the walls of the mountain were too steep, so he had no choice but to keep going.

By the time he reached the small town of Raton, a community of no more than twelve hundred or so it was nearly six o'clock and already dark out.

He saw a lantern hanging in front of the livery barn and headed for it. The hostler, a man of around forty who stood a little over six feet and had the shoulders and arms of a wrestler was standing in the doorway with a coffee cup in his hand. He had on a leather apron that looked like it had seen better days. The big sign over the door said, "Horses boarded, Shoed and Doctored"

As Clay rode up, the man stepped aside and motioned for Clay to enter. "Kinda wet ta be travelin', ain't it, mister?"

Clay stepped down and pulled off his slicker. "Man gets caught out in the open he don't have much choice. I hunted for some shelter but didn't find any."

The man chuckled. "Not between here and Trinidad there ain't." He set his cup down and stuck out his hand. "Walt Slicker, chief cook and bottle washer of this here fine establishment."

Clay grinned and shook his hand and introduced himself.

The man looked at the horses and said, "Fine lookin' animals. Dollar ah day and that includes grain and hay. You brush'm down and I'll tend ta anything else they might need, like shoe'n or doctorin'. As for you, there's hot coffee on the stove in my office and it's free."

"Sounds fair enough," Clay said, looking around for a couple of empty stalls and found only three.

Over coffee, Clay looked at the hostler and said, Go ahead and shoe both horses. They have already come ah fur piece and still have several hundred miles ta go. And while you're at it, check'm over. I'm sure they're healthy enough, but it never hurts ta have somebody who knows, take a look att'em."

"Will do. When do you plan on headin' out?" the hostler asked.

Clay scratched the back of his neck and said, "I was kinda hopin' the rain would let up and I could get outta here come daylight."

"You might get lucky, but I doubt it. This time of year, it can last for days, and maybe even turn inta snow. And if that happens, you don't want ta be tryin' ta find your way down off this mountain. Snow could get several feet deep in no time. Hard ta see a trail in weather like that."

Fortunately for Clay, it didn't turn to snow, but the hard rain kept up for three days and Clay was fit to be tied to get on down the trail and off the mountain. He'd finished the book about the man and the great white whale and wondered what it would be like to ride a ship on the high seas. Maybe someday he would take a trip to California and see the ocean, maybe even take a ride on one of them big ships.

Down in the lobby, the morning of the fourth day, he traded his book for one by a fella named, Washington Irving. The hotel clerk said that in his opinion, Irving would wind up to be a great American author, and went on to say the man was a master at satire. The name of the book was, A History of New York.

Clay told the clerk a little about Herman Melville and his book and the man said he thought it sounded like it would be an even trade.

Up in his room, Clay had just stretched out on his bed to begin reading when a shaft of sunlight hit him squarely in the eyes. He jumped up and ran to the window and saw the rain had stopped.

The big hostler grinned when he saw Clay toting his gear in through the front door. "Bet you're anxious ta get on down the trail, ain'tcha?"

"If I had ta stay another day, I think I'd go stir crazy. I got ah ranch that needs tendin'."

"Your horses are ready - both of 'em fine animals. You wouldn't want ta sell the black, would ya?"

"Not for all the gold in California," Clay said with a grin. "What do I owe ya?"

The hostler went into his office and came back out with a bill. "Fifteen dollars. Six dollars for board, eight dollars for shoe'in both horses and one dollar for the vet fee."

Clay paid the man, saddled the black and loaded the buckskin and was on the road in less than ten minutes.

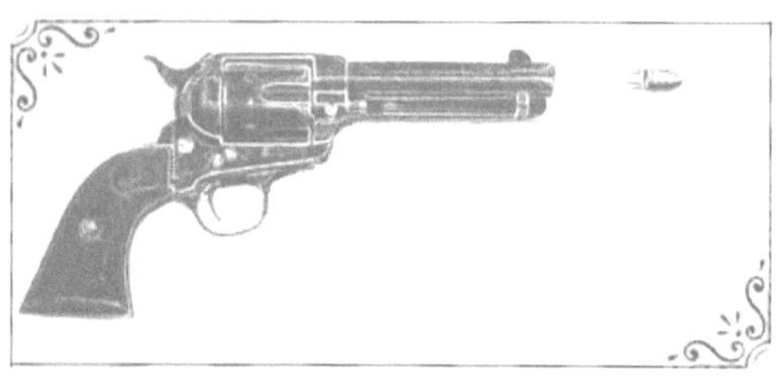

CHAPTER SIXTEEN

-

Clay figured he had a good four-day ride on down to Clayton, New Mexico, which was just shy of the Texas border. If the weather held he should be all right. From Clayton, it would be a short ride and he would finally be back in Texas, and then down to Amarillo, where he would get supplies for the last leg of the trip.

The sun was shining brightly and drying out the ground, which helped make the trip a mite easier. Going downhill on wet or muddy ground was tricky. Your horse could lose his footing and if he went down, there was always the chance he could break something and then a man would be at the mercy of Mother Nature and she could be a bit contrary sometimes. Fortunately, he had two horses, but hated the thought of losing either one of them.

Around noon, the wind began to blow, cold and sharp. Clay was glad he had the sheep lined coat, hat and gloves.

The first night, Clay found a cut between two boulders that led back into a small place out of the wind. There was a small seep of water for the horses. He built a fire under an overhang that would keep any rain from drowning it, should there be any.

Since it was still relatively early, Clay put on a small pot of beans and cut up some jerky and tossed it in, along with a couple of jalapeno peppers and an onion for flavor. While he was waiting for the coffee to perk, he made some pan bread to go with the beans.

There wasn't any grass for the horses to speak of, so he gave each one some corn from a sack he carried on the pack for such times.

After supper, Clay cleaned up his pans, then lit a cigarillo and leaned his back against the boulder, looking up at the night sky. Clouds were racing across the sky like they were late for wherever it was they were headed. From time to time, he could see a lone star looking down toward the earth like it was searching for somebody to be friends with.

He added dry sticks to the fire and got his new book out of the saddlebag and climbed into his soogun and began to read the opening.

It was written by this man, Washington Irving, but the book was narrated by this fella he called, Diedrich Knickerbocker. The man at the hotel said he also had another book by this Irving fella, called The Legend of Sleepy Hollow, but hadn't read it yet.

Clay knew a little about history and thought the title, The History of New York, sounded interesting, but after an hour, he decided the author sure knew how to take liberties with the truth and spread it on thick. This Irving fella sure had a vivid imagination and he was enjoying the story, but before long, he felt his eyes grow heavy.

The sound of rain and wind brought Clay awake. It wasn't raining hard, but the wind was blowing it in under the ledge. Rolling out of his soogun, he knew there would be no time for coffee this morning; he had to get down off this mountain.

As he rode back down onto the trail, thunder rumbled and the clouds were so black it was hard to tell if it was daylight yet. The wind against his back had a bite to it and getting colder.

Even though Clay was anxious to get down the mountain, he knew to give Midnight his head and let him pick his way down the trail. He was wild born and had a better sense about his footing than Clay did.

The black stallion must have felt his master's urgency, or maybe he sensed there was a storm chasing them, but whatever it was, he wasted no time; nor did the buckskin packhorse.

Although Clay was hungry and knew the horses were also, he didn't stop for the noon meal because not only had the wind gotten colder, the rain had changed to sleet. He needed to get off this mountain and find shelter.

By late that afternoon, he reached the bottom of the mountain and had still found no place to get in out of the storm that would allow him and his horses the protection they desperately needed. Sleet ice was caked on the back of his slicker and also on the haunches of his horses.

Another quarter of a mile down the trail, Clay thought he saw something off to his right that looked like a shack or rundown house and turned the black stallion in that direction.

The place sat back in a small clearing, somewhat protected by the hill just behind, and on both sides of it. There was also a small barn and a corral that was empty.

Clay rode up to the house and called out, "Hello the house!" but there was no answer. Next, he rode out to the barn and stepped down. As he started toward the barn, both horses started dancing around and acting nervous.

"Whoa, there. It's just ah barn and maybe there's some hay inside," he said, patting the black on the neck, then turning, he walked to the door of the barn and swung it open. He was just about to go inside when Midnight whinnied and Clay turned his head to see what was wrong.

At that moment, he not only heard what sounded like a thousand rattlesnakes all sounding off at the same time, but also felt a set of fangs penetrate his left boot.

Jumping back, he put his right foot on the snake's back, just behind his head and jerked his left foot loose. Then with his knife, he reached down and cut the snakes head off. Both horses had backed off several feet from the rattlesnake and were pawing the ground with their front hooves.

Clay knew he had to get in out of the storm and see to his foot, so, trying to stay calm, he hobbled over to the shack and slowly opened the door. It was dark inside and he could see nothing. After the incident at the barn, he was taking no more chances and reached down and picked up a rock and tossed it inside, which caused another eruption of rattles.

Clay stepped back and closed the door, then walked over and scouted around. Close to a giant rock just to the side of the shack and somewhat out of the wind, he saw a spot that might work. Finding no snakes, Clay whistled and Midnight and the buckskin came walking over to him, still quivering. Horses have a fear of rattlesnakes and with good reason, especially horses who were born in the wild like Midnight and the buckskin had been.

"Easy now," he said to both horses. "There's no snakes over here. They're all in the barn and the shack, stayin' outta the cold weather like we'd like ta do. Its what snakes do in the winter. It's called, hibernation." His soft words seemed to calm them down.

Clay knew he didn't have much time before he would start to feel the effects of the snake bite, so, still without exerting himself any more than he needed to, he stripped down the horses and let them feed on the grass growing close to the boulder. He didn't bother picketing them; they wouldn't go far, not in this storm.

Clay had just finished putting coffee to boil when he began to feel nauseated. He was fairly sure if he didn't panic, the poison would filter slowly through his system and make him sick, but wouldn't kill him. Panic and running around like a chicken with its head cut off was what rushed the poison to your heart and caused you to have a heart attack. It was the heart attack that killed you, not the poison. On top of that, he figured with the thickness of his boot, the snake had barely penetrated the skin and hadn't given him a full dose; at least he hoped that was the case.

Between feeling sick and throwing up, Clay fought the urge to go to sleep and somehow was able to drink a little coffee and keep the fire going.

After a few hours, he wasn't exactly sure just how long, he began to feel better and was able to put a meal together. He needed to eat something if he could, so he made a broth out of boiling water and pieces of jerky stirred in. It tasted good and helped calm his stomach some. He felt weak, but figured the worst was over and he would live.

He was mighty tired and some weak after his ordeal with the snake and knew he would need some rest, soon. The storm was still raging twenty feet from where his camp was and the horses had their hind quarters turned in that direction.

Clay forced himself to stand up and hobbled over and put blankets over the horse's backs. It wasn't much, but it should help, especially if he could keep a fire going.

That night, wearing his sheepskin coat, hat, and gloves, he wrapped himself in his soogun and sat with his back against the boulder, hoping he would wake up ever few hours to add wood to the fire.

When he opened his eyes, Midnight was standing next to him with his head down close to Clay's face.

At first, he was startled, then recognized his horse and said, "Mornin'. Are you tellin' me it's time ta shake ah leg?"

Midnight shook his head up and down and pawed the ground.

Clay sat quiet for a moment, to see how he felt. He'd not taken off his boot for fear his foot would swell and he wouldn't be able to get it back on. His foot, where the snake had bitten him was sore, but other than that, he thought he felt all right.

He stood up slowly and looked out beyond their camp. The storm had passed and the sun was shining brightly. In the daylight, the shack and the barn didn't look near as daunting as it had last night, but he knew the danger was still there. He just hoped no one else wandered in here during the middle of the night.

Two days later, Clay rode off the mountain onto rolling green hills, lush with grass and cattle as far as the eye could see. He knew he was still a little over five thousand feet up, but it was a drastic change from the rugged mountain behind him. Not far ahead he saw Rabbit Mountain and knew Clayton, New Mexico wasn't much farther.

The area had been used by large cattle and sheep ranchers since the early 1800's because of its wide-open spaces and good grass and water, but then in 1887, one of the big ranchers, he couldn't remember who, established the town of Clayton to be used as a railroad shipping station for his own cattle, along with drives coming up from the Pecos and Texas Panhandle areas.

As Clay rode into Clayton, he saw a small sign swinging from some leather straps that said, "Doctor," almost hidden in amongst the larger, saloon, hotel and restaurant signs.

Clay was sure he was all right, but knew he would feel better with a doctor's opinion.

"You were lucky," the old doctor told him. "And it's a good thing you didn't panic, otherwise, you'd a died up there."

There were two small red spots still on the top of his foot that the doctor cleaned and put medicine on, then, after checking his heart and eyes, declared Clay fit to travel.

His foot was still a little swollen, but otherwise he felt fine, and he was able to put his boot back on.

Had he had the time, he would like to have stuck around for a few days and talked to some of the cattlemen and maybe even a sheepherder, about prices and such. As it was, he was determined to get an early start in the morning.

At the livery stable, Clay bought another horse, a gray mare with white mane and tail, who stood sixteen hands and was told by the hostler that she could run all day and half the night and still not be tired.

Clay wasn't sure that was accurate, but she did look to be in good shape and seemed to have plenty of spirit.

Even if he rode steady, it was still a five-and-a-half-day ride to Amarillo. From Amarillo, it would take another twelve to fifteen days to reach the White River - then several more days following the river down to his ranch. A second riding horse made sense.

After seeing to his horses, Clay stopped in the saloon for a beer and hopefully a little conversation before going to supper at one of the local restaurants.

The saloon was crowded as a cattle drive had just come in and the cowboys were thirsty and letting off steam.

When the bartender brought Clay his beer, which was cool and frosty, he took a sip and turned to the cowboy standing next to him. "You with the trail drive?" he asked friendly like.

The cowboy looked at Clay with contempt, "What's it to ya?" he asked as though Clay had said something wrong.

"Not ah thing," Clay said. "Just makin' conversation."

"Well make your conversation with somebody else, stranger," the cowboy said.

Clay looked at the young man and wondered why he was so rude. He stood close to six feet tall and looked to be in reasonably good health. "Fair enough," Clay said and picked up his beer and started to walk away.

Clay was wearing his sheepskin coat and the young cowboy reached out and grabbed him by the shoulder, spinning him around, causing him to spill his beer. "As ah matter of fact, why don't you go find another saloon, one that caters to you stinkin' sheepherders? We don't allow'm in here."

For some reason, maybe because he'd been on the trail for several days or maybe because he'd been bitten by a rattlesnake and lived, he didn't know. But he did know he was suddenly in no mood to be treated this way.

He tossed what was left of his beer in the cowboy's face, then drove his right fist into his gut and heard him expel a gust of wind. Then he grabbed him by the hair and thumped his forehead against the bar three times, before standing him up straight and slapping his face several times.

"Maybe it's you who needs ta find another saloon, or better still, go on back where you came from and learn some manners before you venture out among men." And with that, he grabbed the young cowboy and escorted him to the door and sent him sprawling into the street.

When he turned around, three cowboys were standing side by side with their hands hovering over their pistols, ready to brace him.

Before any of them even thought about pulling iron, they were looking down the barrel of Clay's big forty-four.

"Don't even think about it," Clay said in a calm, relaxed voice. "Where I come from, and it's not sheep country, although I got nothin' against sheep, we learn a little somethin' about a man before we run off at the mouth and jump ta conclusions or make false accusations. You might want ta tell your friend that when you see'im, if you do."

The three young men just stood there, licking their lips, thanking their maker they hadn't gone off half-cocked and drawn on this man, whoever he was.

"Now, you can go on about your business and we can be friends, or you can die where you stand, your choice," Clay said, putting his pistol back in its resting place, dropping his hand down, ready for action.

"The man on the left, shook his head and said, "You won't have no trouble from me, mister, and I'd be much obliged if you'd let me replace that beer Charlie caused you ta spill."

One of the others turned back toward the bar. "You'll get no trouble from me, either. Charlie had a little too much to drink, that's all."

The third man, stared hard at Clay, then walked past him and out the door.

"He gonna be trouble?" Clay asked as he walked up to the bar and accepted the beer the cowboy handed him.

The cowboy who'd bought the beer, took a sip and looked toward the door. "Don't know much about him, he's new. Got hired cause he's ah friend of Charlie."

Clay let that piece of information find a small place in his memory and settle in. "You can tell Charlie, I'm not lookin' for any trouble, but I won't run from it either. And just in case he's interested, and decides he still wants ta tangle with me, let him know he'll be tanglin' with ah Texas Ranger," Clay said, dropping his badge on the bar for them to see.

"I'll be sure and tell them both," the cowboy said as he finished his beer. When the other two cowboys finished their beer, they nodded at Clay and left.

Clay heard one of them exclaim as they left the saloon, "Ah Texas Ranger. Charlie is lucky ta still be alive."

The bartender sat a second beer on the bar in front of Clay and said, "Thanks. That could have gotten ugly."

"I'm basically ah peaceable man and I for sure don't go lookin' for trouble; too much of it shows up unbidden. Besides, I'm just passin' through."

The bartender nodded and moved on down the bar to tend to an elderly man who came in and stood waiting for his drink.

Clay downed his beer and left.

CHAPTER SEVENTEEN

Clay was anxious to hit the trail, knowing he still had a long way to go, and the next leg would be crossing a barren piece of land known as the dust bowl. Shelter and water would be scarce for the next hundred and thirty miles, where he hoped to reach the Canadian River. He could follow it on down to Amarillo with plenty of shelter in among the trees and plenty of water for the horses.

After a good supper, a decent night's sleep and a big breakfast, Clay was ready to hit the trail. Both he and his horses were rested and there had been no more problems with Charlie or his friends.

The sun was scorching hot by noontime when he traded mounts. The sky seemed to be endless and was clear blue with an occasional small white puffer here and there, but no sign of a storm, which gave Clay added hope.

By late afternoon, he'd crossed over from the New Mexico Territory into Texas. The sun was still a blazing orb settling into the west when Clay found a wash with a small pool of water for the horses.

Looking around Clay saw nothing but heat waves dancing across the land along with an occasional dust devil. It was a barren wasteland as far as he was concerned. Out here in the panhandle of Texas there was nothing but miles and miles of nothing but miles and miles. How the Indians could be happy living out here he wasn't sure, although he remembered his father telling stories about the Indians and their ability to survive here.

As a young man before meeting Clay's mother and settling down, his father had been part of an exhibition to explore this part of the country and told stories about how they had lived with the Indians for a short while and what wonderful people he thought they were.

Clay pulled the saddle and the pack off the horses and let them drink their fill while he wiped the sweat from their backs, neck and face with a piece of burlap before they took a roll. There was not enough grass for them to eat, so he'd have to use some more grain from the pack.

Although he hadn't seen hide nor hair of anyone, that didn't mean he was alone. This was, after all, Indian country - mainly Comanche. Back in his father's day, they had been friendly, but according to his father, the white man came in and tried to destroy them and their way of life – and they fought back. Even though they had no chance of winning against the overwhelming numbers of white men, they could be on a man before he knew they were anywhere around. Many a white man had lost his hair out here without firing a shot.

There were no trees for firewood, but he did find some dried buffalo chips and made do.

By the time supper was finished and he'd cleaned up his dishes, the night was filled with at least a million stars and the moon was so big and round he thought he could reach out and touch it. The night brought a cold wind, which wasn't uncommon. Most of the time the days in this part of the country were hot and windy, and the nights cold enough to need a blanket.

Rolled in his soogun, he slept comfortably through the night without any dreams - the first time in quite a while.

The following morning, Clay was on his way before the early morning dew had a chance to dry. The land was flat with a few small hills here and there.

Gray clouds covered most of the sky, making the air cooler. Because of this, they made good time. At noontime, he stopped for coffee and to change horses.

He made a small camp right out in the open, hoping he wasn't being watched. When his coffee was ready, he lit a cigarillo and stood looking at the sky. The clouds had turned black and there was a change in the wind. The temperature dropped suddenly and Clay saw the large snowflakes, the size of a twenty-dollar gold piece, beginning to fall.

By the time he stepped into the stirrup and swung his leg over the buckskin, snow was already beginning to cover the ground and all around him the ground was white.

A northern, he thought to himself. At least that's what he'd heard them called. He'd never actually been in one but he'd heard stories. Back in Kansas, they were called blizzards and he'd seen plenty of those. They came sudden like and sometimes lasted for days or even weeks.

By the time he'd gone just a few miles, it was getting hard to see and since everything looked the same and there was no sun to guide him, he wasn't sure he was even going in the right direction.

Straining his eyes, Clay tried to see a place where he might get in out of the storm, but he could see only a short distance because of the heavy snowfall. The temperature was continuing to drop and the wind was getting stronger, blowing the snow into drifts.

He knew he had to find shelter of some kind or both he and his horses would die. He'd heard freezing to death wasn't such a bad way to die; you just went to sleep and never woke up – but he had no desire to find out if it was true or not.

The buckskin came to a halt and Clay looked over her head to see why. There on the ground was what looked to be a man lying face down on the ground and a woman on her knees, next to him.

Clay stepped down and made his way toward them, but stopped when the woman stood up – a small bundle in one hand and a knife in the other.

Clay could see she was a Comanche squaw, and she was holding a baby.

Thank goodness for the three Comanche Indians who worked for him. They had taught him to speak the language, which would come in handy now if he was going to be of any help.

"I am a friend. I will do you no harm." Waving his arm around, he said, "We must find a place to get in out of this storm. May I see ta your man?"

The young squaw looked at Clay for a minute; surprised a white man could speak their language. Then, after a moment, she lowered the knife and nodded her head.

Clay knelt next to the young brave and saw a red spot on his back. He was unconscious and his breathing was shallow. From the large stain on his shirt, it looked like he'd lost a lot of blood.

Raising his shirt enough to examine the wound, Clay saw that the bullet had gone all the way through the muscle just below his left shoulder. He didn't think anything vital had been hit but the young man needed tending to.

Clay looked up at the young squaw and asked, "Is there any place close by where we can get some shelter?"

She raised her arm and pointed, but when Clay looked in the direction she was pointing he saw nothing but heavy snowflakes.

Trusting to her knowledge of the land, Clay lifted the young brave and laid him face down over the saddle of the buckskin, then helped her up behind to hold him in place – then swung up on the black, riding bareback.

Clay rode up next to her and indicated she led the way.

A few minutes later, Clay could barely make out what looked like a small hill and when they got to the backside there was a place approximately twenty feet long and ten feet wide where there wasn't any snow, yet.

It was far from ideal, but it was better than being out in the open. Clay wasted no time making a fire from the buffalo chips he had collected and put on some water to boil for coffee and to clean the young brave's wound. Clay also made a pallet for the young mother and her baby, back against the wall of the hill, where they would be out of the wind, but still able to feel the warmth of the fire. He gave her a blanket to put around herself and the baby.

After tending to the young brave's wound and dressing it as best he could, he carried him over and sat him upright against the wall of the hill, close to his wife and child, then went back and began making some broth from melted snow and jerky to feed the young man when he came to, if he did – along with a pan of bacon and beans and pan bread for himself and the woman.

While their supper was cooking, he tended the horses – putting blankets over them to help stave off the cold and feeding them some grain. He had to be careful how much he gave them because he wasn't sure how long they would have to stay here.

Turning back, he took a large pan and scooped up more snow and put the pan next to the fire. This he would use to give the horses, water.

When the food was ready, he took a plate to the young woman, who ate like it had been some time since her last meal and then held out the plate for more. Fortunately, Clay had made plenty.

Outside, night was upon them and the storm was raging fiercely while the hill braced its back against the driving force of the wind, and kept most of it at bay.

Clay had just added a few more chips to the fire when the young brave suddenly leaned forward, eyes wide open, fear showing on his face.

When he saw Clay, he tried to rise, but didn't have enough strength and slumped back down.

Clay spoke to him, but too late, he'd already gone back to the place of darkness.

The young squaw left her baby wrapped in the blanket and went to the fire and got the broth, then knelt next to her husband and ladled the hot soup into his mouth as best she could. Some ran down his chin and onto his chest, but she saw him swallow and knew he was getting at least some nourishment.

After tending her husband, she stood in front of Clay who had been standing to the side, and said, "Thank you. I do not know how you know our language or why you help us, but I will not forget."

And with that, she went to the fire and added more chips, then wrapped back up in the blanket and held her baby close to her.

Clay watched her. She was strong, this one. Of course, Indian women had to be strong, but would that be enough. Blizzards in this part of the country could come on without any warning with the temperatures dropping to below zero and snow drifts shoulder high to a horse. He couldn't even imagine how many people had died in blizzards over the years. If they got out of this one alive, they would be lucky.

For five days, the storm raged without any letup. And for five days the young brave was in and out of his delirium where he yelled and tried to fight some unseen foe and it took both of them to hold him down. Clay was convinced these dreams were caused by a high temperature and after each occurrence; he bathed the young brave's face with snow he scooped up in his hand, which seemed to allow the young warrior to rest for short periods.

As each day passed, Clay's strength was ebbing from trying to stay awake to make sure the fire didn't go out, along with doing the cooking and keeping watch over the young warrior, changing his bandage, daily. The young squaw helped as much as she could, but most of the work fell to Clay, since the baby took up most of her time.

Clay had only his coat, hat and gloves to keep him warm because the young brave and his squaw, and the horses were using all the blankets. As long as he stayed near the fire he was all right.

He knew their fuel would run out soon and wasn't sure what he would do then.

During the quiet time, the young squaw would come and sit next to him and they would talk and learn a little about each other. She was called, Antelope, and her husband was called, Wolf. Their baby had yet to be named but she hoped they could get back to their people soon so the naming could take place.

She told him it had been time for her husband to go away from the tribe and meditate and she had gone with him. While they were out on the plains, the baby had come and they had started back when they had been attacked by the white buffalo hunter who shot her husband and was about to rape her, when he saw the baby and left. And then the storm had come and she thought it was time for them to die, but he had showed up, and she was thankful.

She also told him one thing that helped her to not be afraid, was because he looked a lot like her uncle, Walks Tall.

Clay had heard stories that everybody had a look-alike out there, somewhere, but found it funny that his might be a Comanche Indian.

The buffalo chips were beginning to run low and Clay was worried about what they would do if the storm didn't let up soon. With no fuel, they would eventually freeze to death.

The evening of the fifth day, the storm began to ease up. It was still very cold, but the snow had stopped falling and the relentless wind had died down. Clay could see a few stars trying to peek through the clouds and felt hope.

He was sitting with his back against the wall of the hill, trying to get some rest. His eyes were heavy and he was having a hard time holding them open and felt himself slipping into a state of much needed rest, when his inner senses, the ones that are always on the alert for danger, suddenly told him to wake up!

He opened his eyes just in time to see the young brave standing over him - swinging something at his head. He tried to turn away, but was too late and felt a blinding pain when the blunt instrument struck him in the head, then, nothing.

CHAPTER EIGHTEEN

-

When Clay opened his eyes and looked around, he was alone, lying next to the side of the hill, his body trembling from the cold. Even though it was daylight, the sky was dark and heavy with cloud cover and it was snowing. How long he'd been asleep he didn't know, but it must have been for some time because the wind had blown snow into the area where the small clearing had been.

Where was he and how had he gotten here?

Sitting up, he felt a stabbing pain on top of his head and when he reached up, he found dried blood, along with a large bump that was very tender.

His teeth were chattering so hard he was surprised they didn't break. Why wasn't he rolled up in a blanket or wearing a coat? Nothing made sense, including the fact that he suddenly realized he didn't know who he was or what he was doing here.

Struggling, he got to his feet, and with one hand on the wall of the hill he made his way a few feet away and looked out across the snow-covered landscape. There was nothing to see but endless white. Shouldn't there at least be a horse or a wagon, or something?

He turned and saw where a fire had been, but now it was out and he saw nothing with which to start it up, again.

Looking around, he knew he couldn't stay here. With no heat or food or warm clothes, it wouldn't be long before he froze to death. But where could he go and how, other than walking, could he get there?

In the far distance, he thought he could see a hill and wondered if there might be someone there who could tell him who he was and what he was doing here. He took a deep breath and looked down at himself. He had on a shirt, pants and boots, not much protection to go traipsing out into a blizzard, but what choice did he have.

For some reason, he felt something was missing and couldn't figure out what it was until he started to walk, and then it came to him, he didn't feel weight against his right leg. Did he wear a pistol rig?

Suddenly, he got very dizzy and had to sit down for a few minutes to let his head clear. He knew he couldn't stay sitting here much longer. He had to at least reach the hill in the far distance in hopes he could find so people or something to build a fire with.

With great effort, Clay made his way back onto his feet and started out. "Just keep puttin' one foot in front of the other," he kept telling himself.

The going was slow and he could feel himself getting weaker from the cold; plus, his head was hurting something terrible. He had stabbing pains with each step.

It was difficult walking in snow up to his knees on feet he could no longer feel. He was tired and just wanted to sit down and sleep. Only sheer willpower kept him awake and moving forward and that was beginning to fade.

How long he'd been walking, he didn't know, but the hill seemed to be no closer and he could feel his strength getting less and less by the minute. He was no longer cold, or if he was, he was too numb to know it. From somewhere, he remembered reading that freezing to death was the least painful way to die.

Suddenly, you weren't cold anymore and you just went to sleep and never woke up. To just lie down and get it over with was tempting, but the other part of him would not accept giving up.

Suddenly, the world began to spin and he felt himself falling. He put out his hands to grab onto something, but there was nothing for him to grab on to and he landed flat on his back, deep in a blanket of snow.

For some reason, he felt no pain and wondered if this is what it felt like to die? If it was, maybe dying wasn't so bad after all; at least it was painless.

Before everything went black, Clay wondered if there was anyone waiting on him to return from wherever he'd been and when he didn't come back, would they miss him, or come looking for him - probably not until spring. You wouldn't be able to find anyone in all this snow.

"Well, if there is somebody out there waitin' on me, there ain't much I can do about it," he said to no one in particular, and began to laugh, almost hysterically.

All of a sudden, something in him came alive and he didn't want to die. He didn't know what he had to live for but surely there had to be something - but try as hard as he could, he couldn't get to his hands and knees, let alone, his feet.

The pain came to his head, again, and everything went black. Somewhere in the depths of this darkness, dreams took him to places he'd never been – places he'd only read about. He was on a large ship, chasing a great white whale across the wide Pacific Ocean. Cold seawater splashed against his face as the giant whale lifted itself out of the ocean and crashed down on the surface, sending huge waves toward his small ship, rocking it from side to side.

The small ship was getting closer to the great whale. Clay could see one large eye as the whale stared at him. He had a harpoon in his hand that had rope tied to one end of it and he raised his arm, ready to drive the harpoon into the whale's side, when he felt something wet and scratchy against his cheek and he opened his eyes and saw the nose of a black horse, its long tongue, licking his face.

"Go away," he heard himself say from what seemed a long distance away.

After a moment, he heard a voice - a woman's voice. "Wake up, Brentwood, wake up!"

Why would a woman be telling him to wake up, he wondered?

Then he felt hands lifting him.

Why couldn't they just leave him alone with his dreams; he was about to capture a great white whale.

Then everything went black, again.

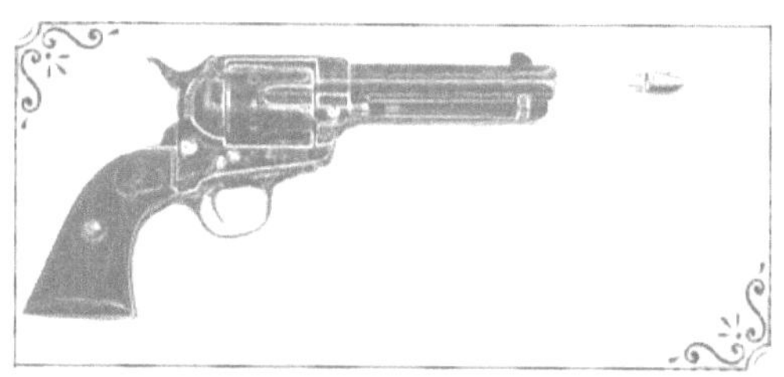

CHAPTER NINETEEN

-

Clay's stomach began to grumble and he opened his eyes, looking slowly around. He was covered with animal skins and inside a structure that was round at the bottom and tapered to a small hole at the top. There was a fire in the middle of the room and the smoke drifted upward and disappeared out the hole.

Something smelled good and he turned his head in that direction.

"Well Brentwood, you have finally come back from the dead," an attractive young Indian woman said.

At first, the statement confused Clay. You couldn't come back once you were dead, could you? He had apparently been asleep, but for how long, he had no idea.

"Have I been asleep, long?" Clay asked tentatively, in the same language she was speaking.

"For six days you have slept, awakened and slept again. You are only still alive because I have forced you to drink broth. But now that you are awake, you must eat meat and vegetables, so you can grow strong again."

She helped Clay sit up and at first, he had a hard time keeping his balance. When his head finally cleared, it was filled with questions.

"You called me, Brentwood. Is that my name?"

"You do not know?" she said as she squatted down next to a pot and scooped some food onto the stiff piece of buffalo hide she used as a plate.

"No. I do not know my name or how I came ta be here. Are you my people? If so, why is your skin darker than mine?"

She smiled as she handed Clay his plate of food and indicated he eat. "No, we are not your people, but we are your friends."

"Then how did I get here?" he asked between bites, savoring the taste of the buffalo meat and the vegetables in a semisweet sauce.

She sat down and folded her knees under her and told him about how he had rescued her, her baby and her husband after the buffalo hunter had left them to die. Then with sad eyes, she explained how her husband had awakened during the night and thought they were Clay's prisoners and hit him over the head so they could escape.

"Thinking he had killed you, he took everything, your horses, saddle, pack, everything. I am sorry, Brentwood," she said. "When we got back, I told my husband the truth about what had happened and he too, was sorry, but since we thought you were dead, we did not go back looking for you."

"Then how did I get here?" Clay asked, handing her the empty piece of buffalo hide.

Antelope giggled. "When we left, I rode the buckskin. My husband, Wolf, said he would take the black stallion for himself, but when he tried to ride him, the horse would not let him. He had to ride up on the packhorse and lead the black one, who fought us all the way. Fortunately, our people were out looking for us and helped bring the black horse to our camp. He is in the corral but still, no one can go near him."

At the mention of the black stallion, Clay knew he should know something about the horse, but for the life of him, he couldn't figure out, what?

Antelope handed Clay a skin with water in it and Clay drank, greedily.

"For almost two days, every brave in the village tried to ride the big horse, but none could. He bit three and drew blood, and kicked several others, then finally he leaped over the barrier where they kept him and ran away," Antelope said, shaking her head.

"That still doesn't explain how I got here," Clay said, not understanding where the story was going.

"I told my husband the big horse was going to look for you, but he didn't believe me, he said horses are dumb and even if it was true, he would never find you in this storm, so I went to my uncle, our chief, Walks Tall, and he found my story very interesting. I wasn't allowed to go with the search party, but my husband did, as well as our chief."

"So, did the horse find me?" Clay asked.

"They said you were buried in several feet of snow and the big horse was standing next to you. He had cleared the snow from your head and was licking your face," she said, giggling, again.

"When they brought you back, you were in very bad shape and I had them bring you here. After all, you saved us from dying and I had to try to do the same for you."

About that time, the flap on the teepee opened, letting in a draft of cold air with snow mixed with it, inside.

Clay looked over and saw two men enter – one of medium height, who looked vaguely familiar and the other one, who was at least a foot taller, Clay guessed would be the chief.

The shorter of the two walked over and stared down at Clay with a happy look on his face. "I am glad to see you live," the brave said, nodding his head. "I am Wolf and I am the reason you almost died," he said with a sigh. "I thought you were my enemy," he said as if that explained everything.

Clay looked at him and saw a sincere face looking back. "It's alright, I probably would have done the same thing had the circumstances been reversed."

The young brave gave a big sigh and said, "You are welcome in my teepee for as long as you want to stay."

"I am Walks Tall, chief of the Buffalo Chasers tribe," a booming voice said.

Clay turned and looked up into a face that reminded him of someone, but he wasn't sure who.

"I am glad to see you are awake and able to talk. When you are feeling better, we have much to talk about."

"Like what?" Clay asked.

Walks Tall looked at Antelope and nodded his head.

Antelope hurried across the tepee and when she returned she handed a broken piece of mirror to Walks Tall, who looked into it then handed it to Clay.

Wondering what was going on, Clay took the mirror and looked into it and then up to the chief, then back at the mirror. Except for the fact that the chief looked close to ten years older, the resemblance between them was astonishing.

The chief nodded his head, "Yes, we look enough alike to be brothers. When you are better, we will talk." And with that, he turned and left.

Antelope took the mirror from Clay, who was still trying to understand. He was a white man and the chief was a Comanche Indian, and as far as he knew, they were enemies.

So, how could they be related?

He knew he wouldn't be able to figure that out until he understood who he was.

Suddenly, he was tired and laid back down and closed his eyes.

It was several more days before Clay could stand without help, and close to a week before he was able to leave the tepee. The air was fresh and felt good in his lungs.

The storm had passed and the sun had melted most of the snow, leaving the ground muddy. Wolf walked beside Clay when he went to see the big black stallion they talked about, and when they got close, the big horse raised his head and looked in their direction, then raced over and slid to a stop in front of Clay and put his head over Clay's shoulder.

Several braves had followed along and were amazed at the black stallion's actions, but not as much as Clay had been.

Clay didn't understand why, but he reached into his shirt pocket and found several lumps of sugar, which he gave one of, to the big horse.

"Do you suppose he'll let me ride him?" Clay asked Wolf.

"If he is truly your horse, and from his actions, I believe he is, he would welcome the feel of you on his back."

Without thinking about it, Clay grabbed a handful of mane and swung up onto his back, then, without a saddle or bridle, he touched his feet to the horse's sides like he'd done this a thousand times.

The black stallion turned and raced across the pen, then, with seemingly little effort, he leaped over the fence and raced out of the camp.

The big horse's head was held high, his tail stood tall and arched, and his mane flowed in the wind as he carried his master across the prairie.

Clay felt something inside him akin to being united with a long-lost friend, and he knew at one time, they had been a team, and would be again.

When he returned an hour later, they all gathered around him and marveled at the black stallion who was covered with lather.

Clay slid from the horse's back and walked toward the corral with the big horse following close behind.

After putting the horse back in the pen that he could easily get out of if he wanted to, Clay wiped him down with some dry grass and talked to him gently.

"One day I'll know your name," Clay said to the big horse who nudged his nose against Clay's chest.

CHAPTER TWENTY

-

Winter was gone and spring was in the air as Clay and several of the braves inched their way to the top of the small rise and looked over the top.

Several hundred buffalo were slowly grazing across the wide valley.

Clay motioned with his hand for them to go back to the bottom of the hill so they could talk.

At the bottom, Crazy Dog was in favor of racing down and shooting as many as they could before they could get away, but Clay raised his hand.

He didn't know how he knew this, but it was his opinion that they circle around and come up, slowly, to the rear of the herd and shoot the ones in the back. "If they don't notice what's happening, they're not as likely to stampede," he said with authority.

Since Clay was considered strong medicine, they did as he said and had downed eight of the buffalo before the herd began to run.

Again, at Clay's advice, they let the herd go and concentrated on the ones they had.

"They won't go far and we can find them, again, if we need more meat and hides," Clay said.

He had downed five of the eight with his Winchester rifle and the noise hadn't seemed to bother the herd, but when Crazy Dog yelled when his arrow struck home, that set them off and they raced away across the prairie for at least a mile.

Clay looked up and saw the women coming with their baskets and skinning knives, and as they passed, several of the women looked up at Clay and smiled.

Clay nodded his head and wondered if one of them would become his woman. Clay still couldn't remember his name or anything about himself and the chief had put off talking to him until he got his memory back.

"What if it never comes back?" Clay asked.

"Then you will become one of us. You will be our brother and there will be no need to talk," Walks Tall said.

They already had a name for him – White Warrior, which Clay knew would change if he was to be inducted into the tribe. But for now, White Warrior would do.

During the months Clay lived with them, he learned many things about the Comanche people. First and foremost, they were not so different from the white man – and in some ways, better, as far as he was concerned.

They loved their family. Children were looked after and taught by everyone in the tribe. And they were loyal. You did not seek another man's woman or you would be killed or turned out of the tribe. Before the white man, they rarely went to war with another tribe.

To them, stealing from another tribe and getting away with it was a game they played. Sometimes horses would go back and forth between tribes many times. And when they fought, most of the time no blood was shed, instead, they counted coup – which meant, touching your enemy and getting away before he could touch you. It was the white man who brought death and destruction, and they learned to be better at it than the white man.

The only reason the white man won was because there was an endless supply of them, and they had better fire power.

By now, Clay wasn't sure he wanted to remember. He liked these people and they liked him. He still didn't know how he knew their language, but it certainly helped.

They had helped him build his own teepee and had bestowed gifts of skins and other things he needed to set up housekeeping. Several of the women had made clothes for him and it was well known that they all thought he should choose a woman to share his teepee.

Clay wasn't quite ready for that, yet. He was content the way things were, but from time to time he still wondered who he was and where he came from – and if anyone might still be looking for him.

Ever so often, something he'd see or do would trigger a picture in his mind, but try as he might, he couldn't bring it to the front part of his brain.

"Maybe you try too hard," Walks Tall told him. "Do not think so hard and if it is to be, it will come – but if not, you are welcome here."

CHAPTER TWENTY-ONE

-

They were all seated at the table and Colleen and Cindy were serving their supper when Riley spoke up. "What if he never comes back?"

Colleen gave him a cold stare. "Hush your mouth. You'll not be ah sayin' such things! He'll be back. He told me he would."

Slim put meat on his plate and looked around at the rest of them, knowing what they were thinking. "We got ta face the facts, Colleen. He's been gone a long time and he ain't been seen hide nor hair of. Even the rangers can't find him. They traced him ta Clayton, New Mexico, then he just up and disappeared."

"You suppose he might'a got caught in that blizzard they had up there ah few months back?"

Running Coyote, who normally said little, said, "It is possible, but Clay knew how to take care of himself and would have made it back by now."

Bert scratched his nose and looked at Running Coyote. "No offense, but do ya think he might'a been captured by Indians?"

Running Coyote sighed and said nothing. As much as he didn't want to believe that, he had considered the fact that it might have happened.

"I think he's just been holed up somewhere, waitin' out the storm, and now that it's springtime, he'll be comin' home," Colleen said with more conviction in her voice than she felt. He wouldn't have let some ole storm keep him from comin' back.

Slim swallowed a mouthful of supper and then took a sip of coffee. "How long do we wait til we get a hold of his attorney and he's declared dead?"

"You really think he's dead?" Riley asked.

"Well, I don't want'a, but he has been gone ah long time and nobody's been able ta find him or come up with ah body."

"If'n he got caught in thet storm whilst he was out in the middle of the panhandle, thet's some mighty lonely country and he might never be found, what with the wild animals out there an all.

They all sat in silence, each wondering if that is what had happened. Each had his or her own thoughts of what would become of the ranch if he was dead, and where would they go?

Colleen did not want to leave here. She'd come to think of the ranch as her home.

In his mind, Running Coyote could not fully believe Clay was dead even though all the facts pointed toward it. Maybe, and it was just a thought, if Clay was dead, would the attorney allow them to buy the ranch?

With Clay not returning, none of them, except Bert, had taken any time off and they still had what money was due them. It might not be a lot, but there was cattle and horses they could sell.

Running Coyote knew that Marion Sooner would help and if the attorney wouldn't sell to them, maybe he would let the Sooners buy it and they could continue to live here and run the place.

One way or another, he wanted to stay here. He'd gotten used to this way of life and didn't want to go back to struggling for existence from day to day.

"I say we give it another month and if he ain't back by then, we can contact the attorney up in Wichita," Slim said, looking around at each of them. They all looked at each other, then finally nodded their heads in agreement.

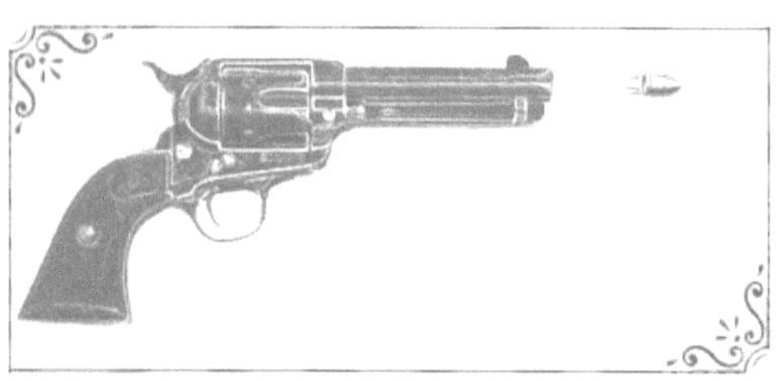

CHAPTER TWENTY-TWO

Clay had pretty much resigned himself to the fact that he would live out his days as a Comanche brave.

He knew they had made raids on several ranches and farms, but they hadn't asked him to go along and he was glad they hadn't because he wasn't sure how he would feel about that. After all, he was a white man and they hadn't done anything to him.

What would he do if the whites raided their camp? What if it was the army? These and other thoughts were constantly a part of him. Even though he tried not to dwell on it, his thoughts always seem to drift to the questions, who was he? Where did he come from? And was there anyone out looking for him? If there was, a Comanche camp would be the last place they'd look. And had the Comanche raided his people, if he had any near here.

That night after the evening meal, Clay, Wolf and Walks Tall sat around the fire, talking. At one point, Clay said, "I have been thinkin' and I wonder if I rode inta a town where white people live, would someone recognize me and tell me who I am?"

"You are White Warrior, and a brave of the Buffalo Chasers and that is all you need to know," Wolf said with conviction.

Walks Tall looked at Wolf and said, "White Warrior and I will walk down along the river. It is time for us to talk."

Wolf nodded to his chief and left.

As they walked along the river, the moon shone down and they could see fish jumping at the moonbeams. The night air was cool, but not cold.

"You have a good life here, White Warrior," Walks Tall said. "But, I also understand how you feel. I myself have had similar feelings."

Clay stopped and looked at him. "You? You know who you are and where you come from. You are not only a brave Comanche warrior, but the leader of your people."

"I would like to believe that," Walks Tall said, "but there are things I, too, wonder about," he said, stopping and staring out across the river.

Clay stopped next to him and waited.

"There is a story that many years ago, a group of white men came to us, wanting to know about us, how we live and other things. They stayed with us for many moons and one of them fell in love with one of our squaws, and she with him. Her name was Blossom. When they found out she was carrying his child, he married her according to our customs and they were happy. Like you, he was a mighty hunter, but when she died at childbirth, he could not stand living among us any longer. Even though he had a son, his grief was more than he could stand. I am told that white man was my father."

Clay stood there, looking at Walks Tall in disbelief. If that were true, then he now knew the reason for them looking so much alike. And that would explain a lot. His father had said he'd lived among the Comanche for close to a year.

Walks Tall looked at Clay and smiled as though he could read Clay's mind. "I believe it is true, we are not just brothers of the tribe, but blood brothers with the same father."

Suddenly, Clay wondered how he knew that his father had lived among the Indians? And then it all came rushing back, his name, who he was, everything, and he began to laugh uncontrollably.

Walks Tall looked at Clay like he'd lost his mind and when Clay could catch his breath, he explained it all to him.

Walks Tall was both glad and sad. He was glad that his brother had regained his memory, but sad at the thought that he might want to return to his people.

"Does this mean you will be returning to your people and your ranch?" Walks Tall asked.

After a moment, Clay said, "I will be leaving in the morning, but tonight, I would like you to call everyone together. I have something I want to say."

The night was full of stars and the fire was roaring as the people sat around it, waiting for White Warrior to appear.

Clay came out of his tepee and walked over to them and they got quiet, wanting to know what he had to say, as Walks Tall had said nothing, except that White Warrior wanted to talk to them.

Almost all had guessed that his memory had returned and, if so, they would be glad for him.

Clay stood looking at them for a moment, then said, "I have come ta love you all like brothers and sisters. You will always be family ta me."

They all smiled and nodded in agreement, for this white man had truly become one of them.

"This very evening, as I stood talking to Walks Tall, we realized we are not only brothers of the tribe, but also, blood brothers, for my father lived among you for many moons and is the father of Walks Tall as well as me. This we have talked about."

There were exclamations and oohs and aahs and much talk among them at such a revelation.

"My memory has returned and I know who I am as a white man. I am happy ta say that my father and I have always been a friend of the Comanche people. My name is Clay Brentwood and I own a ranch many miles ta the southeast of here. There are four Comanche braves who live and work on my ranch as brothers – Running Coyote, He Who Bites, Brave Eagle and He Who Sleeps A Lot."

There were loud exclamations all around the fire for they knew all four of the braves he spoke of.

Clay raised his hands for quiet, then said, "I have sadness in my heart, but I must leave you in the morning and go ta see about my ranch and the people who depend on me, for in my world, I am like Walks Tall, I am their chief."

They all nodded their heads, understanding, but sad to see him go.

Clay held up his hands, again. "There is one thing I want you ta know. If a winter gets bad, you are all welcome ta come and live on my land. You are my brothers and sisters. There may not be buffalo, but there will be beef and you will not go hungry."

Clay and Walks Tall said their goodbyes in private. Unaccustomed at doing so with another male, they hugged, vowing to see each other from time to time.

"Sometimes a fierce storm is a good thing, my brother," Walks Tall said. "Ordinarily, I do not like storms, but if not for this storm, we would never have known one another."

Clay nodded his head in agreement, then clasped hands with his only brother.

The following morning, the entire tribe stood, waving as Clay left them and headed southeast toward Amarillo, riding the black stallion, leading the buckskin and the pack horse.

Fifteen days later, Clay rode to the top of a small rise and looked down over more than a thousand head of cattle, grazing and getting fat on the long-stemmed grass that stretched across his land.

He was grizzled with two weeks worth of beard and leaner by fifteen pounds, but at this moment, he was happier than he had been for a long time.

As he sat there with tears running down his cheeks, he saw He Who Bites ride out of the small grove of walnut trees down toward the bottom of the hill. The Indian stopped his horse and looked in his direction.

For a long moment, they stared at each other, then He Who Bites kicked his horse in the sides with his heels and raced toward the ranch house in the far distance, whooping and hollering.

When He Who Bites charged into the yard and jerked his horse to a sudden stop, raising a cloud of dust, everyone ran over to see what the excitement was about.

He Who Bites leaped from his horse, grinning from ear to ear, and pointed behind him toward the hill.

"He comes."

THE END

FROM THE AUTHOR

Thank you to all my readers. Your reviews and requests for more Clay Brentwood books is an inspiration to me. I'll keep writing them as long as you keep requesting them…

Jared McVay

MEET THE AUTHOR

JARED McVAY is a four-time award-winning author. He writes several genres, including - westerns, fantasy, action/adventure, and children's books. Before becoming an author, he was a professional actor on stage, in movies and on television. As a young man he was a cowboy, a rodeo clown, a lumberjack, a power lineman, a world-class sailor and spent his military time with the Navy Sea Bees where he learned his electrical trade. When not writing you can find him fishing somewhere or traveling around and just enjoying life with his girlfriend, Jerri.

THANK YOU FOR READING!

If you enjoyed this book, we would appreciate your customer review on your book seller's website or on Goodreads.

Also, we would like for you to know that you can find more great books like this one at

www.SixGunBooks.com

Stories so real you can smell the gunsmoke.™